I0708223

Thoreau Lovell

Marco Polo Mother & Son

A Novel

Wet Cement Press

Berkeley, Asheville, Reno

A heart-felt thank you to the readers
of earlier versions of this book: Barbara Roether,
Anthony Schlagel, Linda Rosewood & Lisa Rose.
And especially to the following editors who, each in
her or his unique way, helped me to bring this book
into its current incarnation: Lisa B. (Lisa Bernstein),
John High & Andrea Libin. I literally couldn't have
done it without you.

Contents

Hope Got the Better of Me • 15

Saint Agnes • 37

Men will be Men • 89

Three Pound Hammer • 115

My California • 139

Grief Infinitely Subdivided • 157

You Are Always Welcome • 179

Unexpected Tremors in my Head • 203

List of Photographs • 229

For my mother
Georgiana Helen Mary Allen Lovell Frame
1931-2015

Who will remember me?
Who will remember for me?

—William Kentridge, *Sybil*

Life goes on and on
getting smaller and
smaller until it's
the size of
a seed

Chapter One

HOPE GOT THE BETTER OF ME

[mom]

The older I got the unhappier I became with what I re-membered. Why was this little something lodged in my mind while so many more important things vanished entirely or seemed no more than a dim outline against an opaque sky?

Now I wonder whether I even have a mind for memories to appear in. No mind, no body, no time, but there is something like awareness. I'm aware that I'm here and not there. I'm aware that my son George is wandering through his memories trying to create something like a memorial for me.

I'd like to help him, but he seems to enjoy doing it all by himself. Overdoing it, is more like it. He's trying to write a requiem when a simple pop song would do the trick. More power to him! Whatever that old saying means.

Dwelling on the meaning of words spirals me away from any sense of George or anyone else I ever knew.

So, I step lightly, mindful that remembering is like putting on a play or projecting a movie into a dark room.

There I am sitting at my kitchen table nibbling on a piece of toast, enjoying the hour or so of sunlight that shines through the dining room window in the morning. George is stirring in the spare bedroom. In a few minutes he'll say hello on his way to the bathroom. Disheveled in his wrinkled mismatched pajamas with his thin hair sticking out at odd angles.

George had arrived late the previous night, wearing old blue jeans and a baggy gray sweater with a ratty hood that drooped and clung to his body with no rhyme or reason. He said he left work as soon as he could, but some computer glitch kept him at the library late.

I wonder how he gets away with looking like that at work. How come nobody tells him he's too old to dress like a college student? On the other hand, what's the big deal? Why should I care if my son never learned how to dress like an adult.

By the time George gets out of the bathroom, I have already read the *Fresno Bee* front to back. Once again, I'm offended by the vapid stupidity they pass off as news. I shove the pile of paper toward the center of the table and greet George as he sits down with his coffee. He picks up a section without saying a word.

Oh, my inscrutable son. You never know your children any better than they know you.

For a long time, I regretted naming George after my dad. It just seemed to confuse things. When George was a kid, I couldn't help but look for similarities. My dad who had been a big-hearted funny man who could make anyone laugh. My dad who taught me how to dance and how to ski and how to ride a horse. My dad who was an A1 dresser. And my George, well, my George was different from my dad in nearly every way.

My dad's side of the family was full of Georges. His name was George Edwin, and his dad was George Ernest, and he and my mom named me Georgiana. I'd bet there were dozens of Georges going back hundreds and hundreds of years. When I was young, I was determined not to add another George to the family. Then my dad died, and I got pregnant. And all those Georges from the past started whispering in my ear.

I slide the heavy yellow chair back from the table and stand up. I feel the warm air from the heater pushed down by the ceiling fan. I take three steps to the edge of the counter and wince. The red toaster distracts me, and the faint outline where the wallphone used to hang on the side of the cabinet next to the back door.

I inch my way past the plastic dish-rack and the stainless-steel sink and the basket full of medicines to the cabinet where I keep the glasses. Then I turn and open the refrigerator and pour myself some orange juice. I hate not being able to walk like a normal person. Well, what I hate is the pain in my back when I take more than a few steps. I feel handicapped or disabled or whatever the right word is these days.

When I get back to the table, George is reading the newspaper with his chin resting on the palm of one hand, and his fingers pressed against his cheek. There is a complacent smirk on his face, as if he's reading the paper just to confirm that reading the paper is a complete waste of his time.

Fuck! He suddenly exclaims, sitting straight up in his chair. Sorry, Mom! He quickly adds, as if he needs to apologize to me for saying what we used to call a cuss word.

Listen to this, George stammers:

The house that William Saroyan, famed Armenian American writer, lived in from 1964 until he died in 1981 is in foreclosure and headed for auction.

Can you believe it? George almost yells, full of frustration with the world.

Of course, I can believe it.

How can they treat one of the few truly great people to ever be born in Fresno like that?

What do you expect, George?

He looks at me like he is going to say something, but what can he say? Most people don't give a shit. That's a simple fact.

George quickly glances down at the newspaper and back up at me. According to the article Saroyan's house is on West Griffith. That's close, right?

Not far. I admit.

Let's go look at it. Come on. Finish your coffee, I'm getting dressed.

Are you sure you want to do that? I'm trying to make it sound like getting up and hobbling my way to the carport and getting in George's car and driving the couple of miles to Saroyan's house is a big deal.

When I stand up my head feels light, and I feel wobbly as a wheelbarrow full of bricks.

If we're going, I grumble, I'm going to need a Percocet.

It's a typical November day. Gray mucky sky. Stiff chilly air that makes me cough. This part of Fresno hasn't changed one iota in the more than 40 years I have lived here, except there are a lot more Mexicans and the lawns aren't so green anymore.

George parks in front of a For Sale sign hanging catawampus at the curb. I notice a plaque stuck to the side of the garage with a lot of writing on it. There's a piece of warped plywood nailed over the front window. Dirt for a yard. One tree hanging on for dear life. It breaks my heart.

George makes me get out of the car, even though the Percocet hasn't kicked in yet. A pudgy man comes over and greets us. He has olive skin and a soft voice, small eyes, and puffy cheeks.

Hey folks, I'm Ernie. Are you interested in the house?

George quickly explains that we're only there because of a story in the *Bee*.

I saw that, too, Ernie nods. It's a crying shame. To do nothing all these years and then to let the place get repossessed. It really bugs me! I grew up here. Ernie points at the house next door.

George's eyes light up. You knew Saroyan?

Of course, I knew Mr. Saroyan, or Willy as we called him. He moved in when I was a young boy. He lived and wrote in this house and entertained in that one. Ernie gestured toward the house on the corner. See that window behind the palm tree? Willy would prop it open with a hand-carved table leg and stand at the sink singing Armenian songs while washing the dishes. People said they could hear his booming baritone two or three blocks away. I couldn't understand a word. Still, I felt tears welling up in my eyes when he sang a sad song and laughter bubbling up in my heart when he sang a funny song. It was the strangest thing.

Ernie is a babbling idiot, I think, or maybe he's just overly friendly with a big heart. Either way, I'm not sure I care. My back is seizing up and all I can think about is sitting down in George's car.

Then I remember something, and it's déjà vu all over again like that famous baseball player used to say.

You know, I interrupt Ernie, I was here once before. You must have been a little kid.

At Saroyan's house? George blurts out.

That's right. I drove by on a whim after reading a different story in the *Bee*. You know, famous author says farewell to the spotlight and returns to his sleepy hometown.

Back then the yard was stuffed with fruit trees. And standing in the middle of this orchard as I drove up was William Saroyan himself, watering the garden with a green hose. He was barefoot and his dark hairy legs were dripping wet. He brought the hose up to his lips and took a long drink, eying me as I stopped at the curb. I could see water dripping from his bushy mustache onto his chest. I leaned over and rolled down the window. Before I could say anything, he pressed his thumb over the hose and sprayed my car.

And that was that. The sum total of my experience with the Great Man. But I loved the fact that Saroyan lived here, in a house not very different from mine.

George's mouth hangs open in disbelief. I guess I never told him that story before. Maybe, because Saroyan living nearby didn't change things in the slightest. Sure, I saw him riding his bike around the neighborhood, and I had fun imagining all the conversations we would have had if he stopped. But he never stopped.

Ernie steps forward. That's very interesting, mam. What you said about Willy's yard is true. It was like another world, particularly for us kids. There were cherry trees and apricot trees, nectarines, and peaches. There was a row of pomegranates along the side of the corner house. There were almond trees, pistachios, walnuts, cashews and more. It was as if Willy had shrunk the entire San Joaquin Valley down to the size of his yard.

And there were tons of birds. Ernie added. Yellow ones that showed up in the spring. Green ones that took over the nut trees in winter. Mockingbirds that guarded the house year-round.

I even saw pairs of hummingbirds dancing over Willy's fingers as he sat writing in the yard, as if they were signaling to him which keys to press on the typewriter.

Ernie cuts his story short when he notices me grimacing. Are you okay?

My back is feeling worse, but I am also a little put off by his story. Why bother with the hummingbird business. I check on George. He has a big smile on his face. It doesn't look like he wants to go anytime soon.

Well, Ernie, I answer, I'd feel a lot better if I could sit down.

By this time, we are standing in what is left of Saroyan's backyard. Ernie tugs on the sliding glass door, and it scrapes open. He guides me to a plastic chair next to a white folding table. He gets another chair for George, who sits down, crosses his long legs, and leans back with his hands behind his head. There are pictures of Saroyan taped to the wall and a few of his books lined up on a small bookshelf. I rub my hands together, eying a portable heater plugged into a power strip.

Ernie picks up a yellow notepad and flips through the pages. He stops and looks at what appears to be an outline. Ernie turns on the heater and starts the water for tea. While he's waiting for it to boil, he slides his notepad to the side and looks up at us. A hint of a smile forming on his lips.

I wish things were nicer here and I could walk you through the house. But there's nothing to see in the other rooms except trash and graffiti.

After making tea, Ernie stands up behind the table and presses his hands together. I fold my arms and stare at him, trying to figure out what he's up to. Ernie is wearing a dark blue sweatshirt with a large brown sports coat thrown over it. I can see the top of his purple polka-dot pajamas poking out from under the sweatshirt.

Ernie starts talking in a voice that sounds like an actor trying to figure out how to read his lines. It's kind of confusing at first. I wonder if he is trying to channel Saroyan's spirit, or if he is just trying to get comfortable enough with us to let his real personality come out. Either way is fine with me. The tea and the space heater and the Percocet are doing their jobs.

As you probably know, Willy was quite a gambler. Ernie begins, speaking slowly while looking first at me and then at George. He lost a lot of money, won a lot too. Lost a lot of friends and made a few as well. After he moved back to Fresno and bought this place, Willy arranged for a boxcar to carry the prized possessions he had managed to hold on to from a warehouse in Oakland where they had been stored for many years to the Fresno train station near the Basque Hotel.

The train lumbered into the station and screeched to a stop. The conductor stepped down to the platform and slowly walked over to the first boxcar, wiping sweat from the back of his neck with a bandanna. He climbed up the ladder and slid open the door. Then he leaned out and stared down at Willy.

Better get moving, Mr. Big Shot. Anything left on the train in twenty minutes is coming with me to Bakersfield. The conductor stood off to the side and spat tobacco juice on the ground. He checked his scuffed-up silver watch. Then he pulled a battered Mayakovsky with the poet's head chiseled on the cover out of his back pocket and started reading the Russian poems in a sharp nasal voice. Proclaiming his disdain for misdirected manual labor and the burdensome transport of unnecessary belongings.

I stare at Ernie in disbelief. No way he's the lumpy mama's boy I took him for. Maybe he's a professor at Fresno City College or even at Fresno State. Maybe he's a regular actor or playwright at Roger Rocka's Playhouse in the Tower District.

Ernie keeps talking: Willy climbed inside the boxcar, searching for a particular crate. When he found it, he pried the top off with a large screwdriver and removed a small wooden box. He walked over to the conductor and showed him what was inside. An old fig sitting on a purple velvet pillow.

The conductor spat again and was about to say something. Willy raised his hand, took the pillow out of the box, and carefully unbuttoned it. He removed two Roman coins and a pair of Egyptian earrings depicting an ibis and a hyena and handed them to the conductor, who acknowledged the gift with a flick of his finger.

Ernie stops for a moment to check if we are still with him. George smiles and picks up his teacup from the table. I take the opportunity to ask Ernie if there is a bathroom I can use.

Of course, he responds, I'll show you the way.

What I don't understand, I protest to Ernie as he guides me through the yard toward his back door, is why some rich Armenian doesn't buy Saroyan's house and turn it into a museum or something?

That's the $64,000 question isn't it, Ernie quickly responds, shaking his hands and shrugging his shoulders.

When we get back from the bathroom, Ernie slides the glass door open and waits for me to enter in front of him. He walks over to the table and shuffles through his papers and asks if we'd like more tea.

I am starting to like Ernie. He's enthusiastic and articulate. A great combination in my book. Once we've settled back into our seats with fresh cups of tea, Ernie stands up and resumes his story. He's more animated, moving back and forth behind the folding table, gesturing with his hands, turning his roly-poly body into a sonorous instrument.

A few years after the crates arrived from Oakland, the neighbor next door dies, and Willy buys her house. The one on the corner I told you about. Ernie reminds us. Willy asks some friends to help move his stuff into the new house. He invites me to tag along too. Standing outside his house, we all crowd around Willy, admiring the fancy brown corduroy pants and billowy white shirt he's put on for the occasion. He unlocks the garage, then steps back and asks me if I would be so kind as to open the door.

I bend down, grab the metal handle, and shove it upwards. I gaze into the garage. It's vast and dim and I can't see anything inside. A couple seconds later, the men push me out of the way and start muscling crates and boxes and irregularly shaped objects covered with blankets onto the driveway. Willy directs them to open the largest crate, which contains a shiny black player piano.

This, Willy announces with a flurry, is my long-lost Nubian Princess.

Ernie pauses again, he's starting to sweat, and looks unsteady on his feet. He sits down with a sheepish grin on his face and says, well maybe that's enough for today? What do you think, folks?

By this time, George is sitting straight up in his chair. I'm afraid he's going to start clapping or something. George waves his hands impatiently, encouraging Ernie to continue. Ernie looks embarrassed, but pleased.

Okay, Ernie says, here is the story of the Nubian Princess as told to me by William Saroyan himself when I was a boy of about 9 years old.

It begins when a Belgium theater producer found the piano in a field near Ghent after a Spanish circus fled quietly in the middle of the night. When he came across the piano, it was playing itself beautifully. Janáček and Scriabin. Balinese gamelan and Indian ragas. Balkan folk songs and Chinese laborer tunes. Then the door slid open on the front of the upright piano and a silvery ghostlike face appeared in the mirrored surface and began speaking.

The theatricality of the scene greatly impressed the producer. It felt like he was witnessing an opera of objects and atmosphere. The producer immediately understood how fortunate he was. He desperately needed to generate publicity and funds for a theater piece he was mounting early the following year.

His plan, conceived that very night in the field near Ghent, was to place an advertisement in the leading newspapers of the Flemish world that read:

Offering

A Mystical and magical player piano
capable of conversing with both dead
and living spirits, along with a generous
prize purse, to the first man or woman
who, in a single calendar month, can:

1) Write a novel

2) Get a friend or family
member out of prison, and

3) Yodel while singing gypsy
songs on a high wire.

Thousands of people with unwritten novels ready to burst onto the page paid the 20 Franc entry fee. As did a large number who knew a crusty tidbit of information which if deposited in the right ear would result in a sad and broken friend or family member returning to what was left of his or her life. The money poured in. The theater producer was overjoyed.

At that time in Belgium, it turned out, there was no shortage of novel-writing, Gypsy-song-singing, tightrope-walkers, who knew a thing or two about the criminal justice system.

The hard part turned out to be the yodeling. Have you ever heard someone of French or Gypsy ancestry try to yodel? It's nearly impossible for people who speak and think in those languages. There is something in the sharp Swiss mountain mentality at the root of the European yodel that is absent in the lowland slur of the gypsy-derived artistic classes.

Willy was in Brussels on a reading tour when he saw the advertisement. By that time, he was a famous writer. A famous writer who was broke. When he saw the poster, a bell went off in his head. He was sure he could write novel in a month. And he knew a thing or two about a lot of different people who happened to be behind bars. And he had once written a play about the circus and learned all about flying in the air and dancing across a high wire.

Beyond all of that, Willy had an ace up his sleeve. His love of Hank Williams. Willy instinctively knew that the American white trash hillbilly is blood brother to the gypsy. Not only could Willy yodel while singing gypsy songs on the high wire, he could do so in a seductive southern accent.

The judges knew a winner when they saw one. They unanimously awarded Willy the prize money and the player piano.

My mind began to wander as soon as Ernie started talking about the contest. But George was transfixed. His fingers tapping a mile-a-minute on his leg while one of his feet tried to keep up. His eyes maintained a laser-focus on Ernie, who paused to take a couple large gulps of tea, before continuing.

It took the men all morning to move the Nubian Princess into the corner house. Willy was nervous, worried that they would damage his prized possession. They had to remove the front door before they could maneuver the piano up the stairs and into the hallway. Then they rolled her into the living room and waited for instructions.

Willy was overjoyed. He opened a bottle of Ararat brandy to celebrate. He sang, he danced, he circled around and around the shiny black piano, while the other men sipped their brandy and gaped at him with reverence.

Willy sent them back to get the piano rolls. I faded into the corner. I was just a young boy, not sure if I should be there or not. I watched Willy smiling at the piano like it was his mother recently returned from the old country.

While we waited, Willy explained to me that the piano could read paper rolls like a book. I stared at the piano in wonder. He told me the holes in the paper were like letters on a page and that the piano scrolls were more valuable than the piano itself. In other words, he emphasized, lowering his voice as if there was someone else in the room who might hear him, the song is more important than the singer.

By this time, I'm ready to bet money that Ernie is writing a book, or working on a one-person play, about Saroyan, that he hopes will be his ticket out of Fresno. Ernie the actor, Ernie the storyteller, has charmed me. I start to wonder if he is married or has a serious girlfriend.

George takes a notebook from his backpack and starts writing in it. He asks Ernie if any of Saroyan's famous friends ever came to the house. Then he asks whether Saroyan might have written something just for Ernie and his friends. Something George could take a look at.

Ernie is getting suspicious of George's questions.

I feel sorry for him, so I stand up and announce that it's time to go. I thank Ernie and ask if I could stop by sometime to hear more of his stories.

Ernie looks happy enough to cry.

We drive home without talking, but I can tell George is pleased as punch with what happened. I don't know exactly what he's thinking, but I can almost hear the wheels turning and the gears clanging in his head.

George pulls into the driveway and hurries over to my side of the car. He guides me up the stairs and into to the living room and sits me down on the couch. Then he dashes into the bedroom to grab his laptop, without bothering to ask if I need anything.

He sits down on the orange chair next to the entertainment center and starts typing. He keeps asking whether Ernie said this or said that. I can't help him very much. Or maybe, I just don't want to.

George sits with his legs stuck out in front of him, his face all screwed up, grasping for details one moment, and breaking into a big smile the next. Something about George's almost desperate attempt to write everything down puts me off. I like Ernie as a person, not as some kind of trophy.

Watching George abuse his laptop like that, reminds me of watching his dad, Whitey, bang away on his typewriter. Sometimes the rat-a-tat-tat of that thing really got on my nerves. But most of the time I loved the sound of his typewriter. It was like hearing Whitey's thoughts without having to know what they meant. The sound of pure thinking.

After Whitey died, I thought I might become the writer in the family. For him some, but mostly for me. I had started a lot of things when we were together and a few after he died. But I didn't have his stick-to-it-ness. Besides, I had to work, and I had a son to raise.

I think Whitey would have been proud of George when he started writing fiction. But I have to admit that it scared me. Poetry is harmless enough, but fiction can suck the life out of you. I saw it when Whitey was writing his silly crime novels.

Amphetamines, coffee, cigarettes.

Days and weeks and months at a time.

Then boom, Whitey was dead.

Dead before he knew what he was doing.

George finally closes his laptop and puts it on the sideboard underneath the window.

So, what did you think of Ernie, George?

He's a natural storyteller. I mean, wow! Where did he get that stuff?

How much of what he said do you think is true?

I don't know, George shrugs. Maybe none of it. Maybe most of it, one way or another. I don't think it really matters.

Of course, it matters, George, I reply, astonished at how caviler he's being with the truth.

Okay, if the truth matters so much to you, George shoots back, did you really go to Saroyan's house and see him watering his garden?

I glance at the white bookshelf next to the couch. The title of one of Saroyan's books jumps out at me. *Sons Come and Go, Mothers Hang in Forever.* Of course, Saroyan was speaking from the son's perspective. Probably after his mother was dead and gone and he was still coming and going in the world, and it felt like his mother would be stuck in his head forever. The picture on the cover shows Saroyan standing in an old cemetery, wearing a thick black cap and a light-colored overcoat. His arm wrapped around a gravestone.

Next morning, I surprise George by getting up before 11 a.m. He thinks that means I'm feeling better. But it doesn't. I tell him, I slept so hard it felt like I had died. George stares at me over his coffee, an incredulous look on his face.

What I don't tell him is that most mornings I wake up disappointed and scared. Because one more night has passed, and I didn't win the Died Peacefully in Her Sleep Lottery.

If you ask me, there are no lovelier words in the English language than, *Died peacefully in her sleep.*

George sits hunched over his laptop again. I ask if he can make us some eggs and toast.

Sure, he mumbles. As soon as I'm done here.

Hey, I've got a great idea. I say ten minutes later when George still hasn't budged. Why don't you buy Saroyan's house and hire Ernie to turn it into a museum and run it for you?

George's face turns red.

Come on, it's not that ridiculous of an idea, is it?

No, of course not. He takes his phone out of his pocket and waves it in front of me. Why don't you call Paula? See what she thinks?

It would be a museum, for Christ's sake. You guys wouldn't have to live there!

George is still typing, with a piece of toast hanging off the side of his mouth, when I ask him, so what are you going to do with my house when I die? George looks up and shades his eyes with his hand, like I'm shining a high-powered flashlight in his face.

I figured George would sell my little, old, house, which in the end is exactly what he did. And I was fine with that. He and Paula have a great house in Berkeley, why would they want to keep my place in Fresno?

But for a moment, I let hope get the better of me, and I imagined that George would keep my place.

Turn it into something like a writer's retreat.

A place to get away from his family and his job and his Bay Area friends and just write.

A place where Saroyan's ghost might visit and inspire him. Of course, my ghost would be there as well. And maybe Ernie's too, once his time has come.

Chapter Two

SAINT AGNES

[son]

Paula and I live above the semi-industrial flats, with their small, once-affordable homes and dusty, horizontal light, and below the Berkeley Hills, where twisty streets without sidewalks snake past storybook homes costing unimaginable millions.

Our 100-year-old house sits in a neighborhood of otherworldly gardens and tree-lined streets. The first time we saw it we knew it was perfect. Or could be.

There was an office and work room for Paula. Lily's bedroom had a converted sunporch playroom. Our bedroom was large with windows on two sides and a door that led to a second converted porch that could be my office.

But of course, we would have to add a second bathroom and a deck and remodel the kitchen and remodel the upstairs bathroom and turn the bare-dirt yard into a lush garden. And, before any of that, we would have to burn sage and chant prayers in every room, to dispel the lingering sickness, mental decay, and overall feeling of grief left behind by the previous owners.

Only then could we crack open the paint and get to work obliterating every inch of white and off-white and beige that reminded us of their sad, dissipated, lives. We painted the living room mustard yellow. The dining room mossy green. Paula's office tangerine. The entryway and stairway blood orange. Our bedroom lemon yellow. And Lily's room turquoise.

Our aesthetic was old-world hippie chic. We paired boomer tchotchkes with family heirlooms. A huge macramé wheel, with an antique butter churn; a Polish theater poster with a 19th century cherry wood cabinet; a German witch mask with a knock-off Ames chair.

Lily was the first one of the family to fully embrace the house. She filled it up with her dolls and magnet tiles, and rolls of white paper, and colored pens, and tubes of paint, and toy animals; and an entire three ring circus that fit inside a suitcase. That three-ring circus became our life. And we did everything from take the tickets to feed the lions.

Lily was a running, climbing, jumping, spotlight-hog of a two-year-old who thrived in the chaos—while Paula and I floundered, confused and in shock. Remind me again, we dolefully asked each other. Why did we leave San Francisco? And pay all this money for a fixer?

Fortunately, Berkeley turned out to be a special place. Making so many things easier than they might have been somewhere else. There was a preschool a few blocks away where Lily could hammer nails and saw wood and jump around in the mud like a gleeful piglet. And there were four or five playgrounds within walking distance. New playgrounds with safe climbing structures and padded surfaces. Old playgrounds with concrete slides banking around old oaks, dotted with bloody evidence of scrapes and falls. And there were parks with overgrown trails to explore and trees to climb and creeks to splash around in. And later there was the German International School up the hill.

Paula couldn't believe her good fortune. San Francisco didn't have a German school. Suddenly, there were German mom's and dad's in our life; German holidays and German songs; and most importantly, German attitudes regarding child raising. It was clear, Paula finally felt at home in Berkeley, once Lily started going to the German school. I, on the other hand, had a much harder time adjusting to the life of a German expat in California. In part, because I wasn't German.

My sense that Berkeley was the right place to live was all about Lily. I had been a bachelor well into my 40s. For many years, I said I wanted to be a dad, but I wasn't sure I meant it. Nevertheless, when the moment of truth presented itself, when Paula showed me the pregnancy test strip in her bathroom in San Francisco, and looked up at me with hope and apprehension, I said yes. YES, in all caps.

So, if Lily liked Berkeley, I liked Berkeley. It was that simple. And Lily loved Berkeley. And she particularly loved the German International School, which was housed in a grand Tudor Revival building built in 1925—just two years after a wildfire raged over the summit, stopping a couple of blocks short of what would become our house.

Lily said going to the German school was like going to Hogwarts—without having to worry about the dark arts. I had read just enough Harry Potter to know what she meant. It was a fine old school, elegant and comfortable, like an English country lodge, with a steep slate roof and a large auditorium that had huge arched windows overlooking the Bay and the Golden Gate Bridge.

I wondered what Lily would have thought about the schools I went to in Fresno. Cheap, flimsy structures. Fenced in blocks. Bored and angry kids. Helpless teachers. All I remember is hanging out along the fence line at recess and sitting in the back row during class. I was a sarcastic and unimpressed student until a couple good teachers got through to me.

One morning when I dropped Lily off, I asked her, do you have any idea how lucky you are to go to a school like this, in a city like Berkeley?

She paused for a second, then chirped, yes, before popping open the car door, swinging her polka-dotted backpack over her shoulder, and dashing across the street to where her friends were playing.

I watched her blond ponytail bounce away from the car and felt stupid. What was the point of asking a question like that?

I had just returned from visiting Mom in Fresno. The contrast between life there and life in Berkeley was stark and unsettling. Fresno felt like the urban equivalent of a disposable advertising supplement. While Berkeley felt like an oasis where high-quality versions of everything you'd ever want for yourself or for your family could be found no more than a couple miles away.

How did I get to live in Berkeley? I wondered. I'd been to Spalding Nebraska, the shrinking farm town where my father grew up. Population 592 and dropping. One main street, three bars, a pizza parlor, and a half-empty hardware store. I'd taken my mother to Detroit for her 60th High School reunion. I'd seen her wooden house on Burt Road, near the Rouge River, simple as a cardboard box. And her grandparent's modest brick house on Northlawn, with its sturdy iron fence enclosing a well-kept bed of roses. I remembered my father's parent's red house near Radio Park in Fresno, with its small, stuffy rooms and the dank, sour smell of cigar smoke.

Being there made me feel good, in a complicated kind of way, which had something to do with my grandmother Resa cooking dinner in a double boiler, and her collection of plates commemorating each state of the union hanging in alphabetical order along her dining room walls.

When I think about all those houses now, including my childhood home on Brooks Ave., what strikes me is how similar they are. Ours had been a tenuous middle class to lower-class existence for generations. How did my life become so different from theirs?

After dropping Lily off at school, I drove around the corner and parked. I was in no hurry to get to work, so I got out of the car and started walking. I past alpine chateaus, Mediterranean villas, Tudor lodges, brown shingle bungalows, log cabins even. Of course, they were all fake. Or at least copies. Fantasies transplanted to the Berkeley Hills where they took hold and multiplied.

I passed a wise old apple tree, a demure cherry tree, gangs of London plane trees—equal parts Asian, American, and European. I passed disinterested redwoods. Rebellious oaks. Upstart eucalyptus. And many other trees I didn't have names for.

Wealth breeds wealth. Abundance breeds abundance. Having a lot makes it easier to get more. The gaudy display of money in the suburbs had repulsed me when I was younger. How was this highbrow show of success and taste any different?

I sat on a stone bench in a leafy nook and stared through the trees at the glistening bay. My phone rang. It was Rosa. My mother's next-door neighbor. She apologized for calling, then told me that an ambulance was at my mom's house and that they were taking her to Emergency.

I grabbed a few things and jumped in the car. If I was lucky, I'd be at the hospital in 3 hours. When I reached Altamont Pass, I glanced in the rearview mirror. A beautiful arc of soft gray-blue clouds stretched across the sky behind me.

Then I began my descent, speeding toward a towering mass of brown muck. I shot past a huge gravel pit. A massive semi-truck trailer manufacturing plant. A stark prison facility. I slowed down and called Paula. She didn't pick up. I slowed down a little more and began to prepare myself.

My mother had been in and out of the hospital numerous times over the past fifteen years because of congestive heart failure, which meant her heart was slowing down, wearing out, like a spinning top wobbling more and more slowly. She also had a bad heart valve, severe arthritis, occasional vertigo, a weak stomach and failing memory.

When she turned 80, I breathed a sigh of relief. Sure, I hoped my mother would live another 20 years.

But if she didn't, at least she'd had a long life. That became my goal as well. Get to 80, still healthy, lucid, with a creative spark. After that, I'd take whatever came my way. The long slow decline or plummeting over a cliff. Whatever.

Once my mother turned 80, I stopped nagging her about her health and tried to make her later years as easy and stress free as possible, even if that meant forgoing medical procedures that might prolong her life.

Paula felt differently. One night, she was sitting in bed wearing her grandmother's white cotton sleep shirt, peering at her laptop screen, when she turned and glared at me with one arm raised. Her stubby finger jabbing the air, her thick dark hair cascading down her shoulders, the color draining from her long flat face.

George, listen to this. Christina's 92-year-old stepfather just had his heart valve replaced in LA. It was like an in-and-out procedure.

Really? Which valve?

It doesn't matter. His heart valve. Just like your mother. She tossed the laptop on the bed and sat up so that her soft body shifted into a more commanding position. You need to call the hospital and get her in there. And she needs to cut her salt intake and stop drinking. And take walks around the block every day. With her walker! And she should take foxglove supplements and passionflower and . . .

Maybe, I interrupted her. But what if she doesn't want to? She's 83-years old after all.

No, George. You've got to fight for your mother. And when I get sick you need to fight for me too. Paula was gesturing with both hands now. Staring up at me from the bed. Exasperated.

Ah, I realized, she's scared. If I don't fight with the doctors and the hospital and the insurance for my own mother, what am I going to do for her when the time comes? Paula was still a relatively young woman, in perfect health. But we both knew that could change in an instant.

I don't want anyone to fight for me when I get sick, I informed her. I just want to be left in peace.

Bullshit, George. You're just trying to piss me off.

Maybe I was, I had to admit to myself, as I drove past fields of dried out corn, and gutted orchards of overturned almond trees, and deep green citrus.

Paula called back after I merged onto Highway 5, just past Tracy. I told her what I knew, which wasn't much, and said that I'd call her again as soon as I got to the hospital.

Should I try to find someone to watch Lily? She asked, more concerned than I thought was warranted. Do you want me to close the store so I can be there with you?

I'm not sure yet, I told her, I'll let you know.

Decision making was hard for Paula. She fretted, she got distracted, she forgot, over and over again, what was important. Unless someone really needed her help. Then she leapt into action. Organizing meal deliveries to a family from school after the husband committed suicide, staying with the elderly mother of a friend who needed a weekend off, driving Lily's friend to therapy after her mother passed away from pancreatic cancer. Etc., etc., etc.

You could count on Paula in a crisis. So, I knew she would be there in a heartbeat if I needed her. But I also knew how much she disliked Fresno and driving through the San Joaquin Valley. Bay Area people are like that. There's always contempt in their voices. An unchecked assumption that the San Joaquin Valley is a land of inbred, hard-hearted, troglodytes. A place to rush through or better yet avoid entirely.

I agree, the Valley is as different from the Bay Area as Indiana is from the South of France. But Indiana isn't hell on earth any more than the South of France is paradise.

Suddenly, a wave of red lights snapped me out of my delirium. I hit the brakes and slapped the steering wheel. God Damn assholes! I screamed. My mother is in the hospital! The driver in the next lane was angry and gesticulating too. I yelled in his direction. How can the main freeway connecting San Francisco to Los Angeles have only two goddamn lanes of traffic!

He yelled something back, flashed his bulging eyes in my direction, then turned away.

I picked up my phone from the console. The small blue dot representing my location was stuck at the beginning of a long stretch of red. I knew I shouldn't do it, but I took the next exit.

When I got off the freeway and rolled down the window and smelled the dirt and felt the tractor dust, I started to relax. My mother would be fine.

In some ways it was a relief when she went into the hospital. At home, she might skip a meal here or there, forget to take this pill or that. At home she might never drink enough water, juice, or tea, but always drink too much beer, wine, or scotch.

I drove past packing sheds and fertilizer plants.

A crop-duster airstrip with World War I biplanes and mud-splattered carts and windsocks.

Endless fields of electric green.

Black ripped up earth.

Enormous steel bins.

Pyramids of irrigation pipes.

The road crested a levy and a wild stretch of the San Joaquin River opened up before me, spilling over its banks and forming a sparkling expanse of wetlands. The surface of the water rippled. The sky over watery land gleamed. Everything was going to be alright.

When I was a teenager, I had a job insulating houses up and down the Valley. For almost four years I got up early, threw on some work clothes and drove to the warehouse. I can't remember any of the guys I worked with. Not a single name or face. Except for the owner. An Italian man maybe ten years older than me with curly brown hair and a bushy mustache. His name was Pinto. Like the bean.

After loading the insulation and checking our gear—masks, gloves, drills, measuring tape, chalk-strings, hoses, etc.—we hit the road in a snub-nosed truck with the words *Golden West* painted on the side in huge orange letters.

Some days we headed south toward the oil fields near Bakersfield, or the naval air station at Lemoore. Other days we drove north to farm towns like Chowchilla, Atwater, Turlock, La Grange, or all the way up to Sacramento. We usually did two houses before lunch and one or two after.

I liked meeting the customers. Seeing how they lived. I liked eating lunch in the truck, or in a cheap restaurant. I liked the stupid talk and the silence with the guys. But what I liked the most, what has stuck with me all these years, was the surprising beauty of the San Joaquin Valley.

My mother and her friends went on and on about the coast, the mountains, Los Angeles, San Francisco. For them, the Valley was a blank space on an old map they had no interest in filling in.

But once I started driving up and down Highway 99 and the smaller roads and avenues around it, I couldn't believe what I was seeing. Grapevines laid bare every winter. Orange and lemon and grapefruit trees with their seductive fruit hanging for anyone to sample a few feet from the road. Almond trees bursting into flower when the air was still chilled. Cotton fields that me made me feel like boss man and sharecropper. Peaches, apricots, and nectarines blazing on the branches like suns with entire planetary systems of desire rotating around their juicy stone cores. Mountains that jutted up in the east, jagged, snow covered, sometimes obscured by exhaust and farm dust and smog blown in from the big cities on the coast.

I thought I was working for the buzz of money and camaraderie, but I quickly realized there was much more to it than that. The San Joaquin Valley was extraordinarily beautiful. A place I could never completely turn my back on.

I drove past an old farmhouse for sale that sat at the end of a long driveway lined with scraggly palm trees. A shabby place with flaking white paint, buckled front porch, a tall wooden water tower in the yard. Unremarkable, except for a shiny red Land Rover and three or four well-dressed people standing around it. In a heartbeat, I decided I wanted to buy that ramshackle farmhouse before the shiny Land Rover people got it. How quiet it would be at night! How peaceful in the morning, drinking coffee on the porch! How great it would be writing in the converted water tower!

Then I saw myself telling Paula that I wanted to give up our life in Berkeley and move to the Valley and the bubble burst. Replaced by rivers of toxic run-off and mean-spirited, freedom-fearing farmers, terrorizing us with their oversized pickup trucks.

I slowed down as I drove through Vernalis and Westley and Crows Landing, Newman and Gustine. Each town a little different from the one before and the one after. But each equally grim and heartbreaking. I drove past a string of roads with evocative names. *Deep Well. Boxcar. Fink Road. Sandy Mush.* And the one that for some reason always stuck in my head, *Ike Crow Road.*

I got off the freeway at Herndon and drove the few miles to Saint Agnes hospital. I parked in the parking lot and hurried up the grassy hill into the atrium-like lobby. When the elevator doors opened on the 4th floor, I stepped into the ICU, and recoiled from the glare of florescent lights bouncing off the polished floor. Blindly, I turned left and walked down a short hallway lined with colorful photographs of California landscapes. I turned right and stopped in front of an open station bustling with nurses. Not one of them looked up as I tried to get their attention. This made me nervous. I thought of the ICU as a restricted area and the nurse's station as a kind of security checkpoint. It shouldn't be so easy to cross that threshold. I wanted someone to stop me, to question my reasons for being there, to ask for my papers.

I turned left and walked down a long corridor. The walls were painted light yellow. A wide molded plastic handrail ran along both sides of the hallway. Many of the doors were open. I saw disposable glove dispensers hanging next to extra-large containers of hand sanitizer. I saw ancient men and women, with paper-thin skin and bird-like bones, lying in their beds stiff as mummies. I saw a man my age or younger shuffle alone down the hallway, his silver IV pole at his side, his pale hairy back and dingy white underwear showing beneath an open hospital gown.

I stopped a nurse in the hallway and asked about my mother. She told me she was stable and resting. I pushed open the door of my mother's room. She was asleep, propped up on two or three pillows. Her face bloated and pasty. An off-white cotton blanket pulled up to her neck. An oxygen tube stuck in her nose. Various other tubes and monitor cables tucked under the blanket. The remains of an uneaten meal sitting on a dull plastic tray.

I looked at my mother's face. Her cheeks hung loose, like a papier-mâché mask. Her eye sockets had deepened and the bones around them appeared soft and sunken. She moaned a little and shifted in bed. The light from the window caught her hair.

Ever since I could remember, her hair had been the same warm reddish brown—like burnished chestnut in an ancient illustration, or like firelight seen through a foggy window. For the longest time it didn't occur to me that her hair was dyed. But as I grew older and my hair thinned and grayed and hers stayed the same rich color, I realized I had been living in a dream.

What was I thinking? That as long as my mother looked young, I would stay young as well? That we were in cahoots with some trickster spirit, or mischievous sprite, who had a soft spot for us in her heart?

While my mother slept, I stepped into the hallway and called Paula. Once again, she didn't pick up. I left a message, saying that I hadn't seen the doctor, but the nurse made it sound like everything was alright. When I came back in the room, Mom woke up, disoriented and squinting.

What are you doing here?

Rosa called me.

She closed her eyes. A chime rang over the intercom.

What's that? She stammered.

I think it means a baby was just born.

Poor sonofabitch! She snapped. Glad it wasn't me!

I couldn't help laughing, but the bitterness in her voice surprised me. She fell back to sleep, and I sat down next to the bed, not sure what to do. She woke up a few minutes later and gripped my hand. She told me I needed to feed her cats and water her plants. Then she closed her eyes and drifted off.

The chimes kept interrupting my thoughts. Mom didn't seem to notice, but I wondered: What if the chimes meant that someone had been reincarnated, rather than born for the first and only time? What would my mother say about that?

I stayed at the hospital with her until about 7 p.m., then left. The doctor never showed up.

Next morning, I woke up in my childhood bedroom. Nothing much of mine was left, except for a few old photographs and my university diplomas, which my mother had hung on the wall when they were new and left there to fade and gather dust.

I brewed coffee in the Mr. Coffee that sat on the dryer in the kitchen. I walked outside to get the newspaper. The surprisingly warm air greeted me like a sweet old aunt. My bare feet soaked up the heat from the driveway.

Brooks Ave was only one block long. Seven houses on my mother's side of the street; eight on the other. I counted three gardener's trailers, nine pickup trucks, a couple basketball hoops, and one oversized American flag drooping from a makeshift flagpole.

Rosa and her family lived next door on the left, in a flat white house with a swamp cooler on the roof, and a lush symmetrical tree in their front yard. I bent down and picked up The *Fresno Bee*, slipped off the rubber band, unfolded the paper, and glanced at the front page. I lingered on the driveway, hoping Rosa would step outside. Then I walked up to her door and knocked.

Rosa was glad to see me and happy that I had come so quickly. She told me to let her know if I needed anything. I thanked her for keeping an eye on my mother, which she did even though my mother only ever spoke to her to complain about the loud music she and her husband played whenever they had a party.

I went back inside, checked the time on the clock above the doorway, and laid the *Bee* on the kitchen table. My mother's small ranch style house may have looked dull and unremarkable on the outside, but inside she had turned it into a wonderful crazy quilt of a home. Especially her kitchen. There were violet drawers. Turquoise cabinets. Huge bunches of dried herbs printed on a wallpaper border. Mismatched pots and pans hanging from a heavy wooden beam. Native American wicker baskets spilling over with bottles of medications and supplements. There was a wooden cat nailed above the doorway, with a large head, orange and yellow nose, black whiskers. Next to the cat an aardvark clung to the wall with yellow legs, green and purple armor, orange ears, and a turquoise tail. Above the two animals hung the clock with fruits and vegetables where the numbers would normally be. I loved my mother's small kitchen made infinitely larger by being stuffed full of things that couldn't possibly fit together in the same space and time.

I took the paper and coffee out back to the narrow platform that ran the length of the house and sat down on a white plastic chair. It was a gentle fall morning, warm, with a light breeze, the sky a whitish blue. It was hard for me to believe that my mother wasn't inside, moving through her daily routine.

Get out of bed, shuffle into the kitchen, make coffee. Feed the cats. Sit at the white Formica table. Eat a bit of yogurt, maybe a piece of toast. Wobble into the backyard, sit in this same white plastic chair. Read the paper, enjoy the fresh air, the yard, the garden. Trudge into the kitchen, eat what she called lunch—often no more than a couple of crackers with cheese. Wobble to the computer room, catch up on email and online shopping. Shuffle to the kitchen for the first beer of the day. Sit on the sea-green couch, watch the news, eat dinner, feed the cats again. Shuffle to the kitchen for more wine, beer, or scotch. Trudge back down the hallway to bed, keeping one hand on the wall for balance.

The smallness of my mother's life both frightened and attracted me. I glanced down at the smiling face of a baseball player in the newspaper and jokingly told him that I wanted to be a bum when I got old, just like my mother, with nothing better to do than move small distances and think small thoughts.

I gathered up my dishes and hurried into the kitchen. Next to the sink was a small green chalkboard on which my mother had written:

Pistachio ice cream
broom?
Apple Sauce.

I didn't know my mother liked pistachio ice cream.

I had let myself get distracted and now I had to hurry. I drove down Brooks, turned left on Holt, right on West and right again on Herndon. Everything along the way looked exactly the same as the day before. The same strip malls, gas stations, office complexes, the same acres of parking lots, the same faded mountains barely visible through the haze. In the atrium the same old woman sat at the same volunteer table with the same inviting smile on her face. Everything in my mother's room was also the same. Except my mother.

She lay stiffly on her back, eyes partially open, staring at the ceiling. One of her hands had slipped out of the covers and was dangling off the side of the bed. When I tucked it back in, she didn't move. I said hello and called out her name. She didn't respond. I panicked. Maybe she's dying, or slipped into a coma! I hurried out of the room, looking for help. Stopping a middle-aged nurse coming out of another room.

Don't worry, her vitals are fine. The doctor will be by soon.

When? I pleaded.

She shrugged and walked off.

I went back to Mom's room. I sat down and stretched my legs and tried to read. I stood up and opened the curtains a few inches. I turned on the TV and turned up the sound. I tried all the different channels. After I turned the TV off, I was assaulted by the constant beeping and buzzing sounds of the machines in the room. The chattering nurses just beyond the door. The clattering carts rolling up and down the hallway.

A pretty nurse with an easy smile came into the room. I flirted with her. She barely noticed, but I felt terrible afterwards. I was just bored, I told myself. And worried.

Mom slept through lunch. I tried calling Paula a few times, but she didn't pick up. Time spread out in all directions, and I drifted through the afternoon with no clear thoughts and no idea of what I should be doing. It was well after 5 p.m. when Dr. Bellus showed up.

Hey George, he greeted me.

Dr. Bellus was a warm, gracious, middle-aged man with sandy hair and a thin, athletic body.

I stood up and shook his hand.

He said, your mother had a rough night. Her blood pressure and iron levels are extremely low, her sodium levels high and she is dehydrated. But other than that, he grinned, she's fine. We've given her something to help her sleep. You might as well go home and come back in the morning.

Paula called back while I was walking to the parking lot.

What's the doctor say?

She's dehydrated and anemic.

Is she awake?

Not really.

Look, George, don't get too comfortable there. You need to be on your toes, all the time. Got that?

I'm fine, I told her, don't worry. I wanted to add, that it would be a lot easier to stay on my toes if she'd pick up the phone. But I didn't.

I drove down Blackstone to a Mexican restaurant I liked, forgetting that the route would take me past the Alhambra Trailer Park, where we had lived for a few years after moving out of my grandparent's house near Radio Park. I slowed down, thought about it, then turned into the narrow driveway, idling past the trailers and the few people who were outside.

I tried to remember what our trailer looked like, or any of the people who lived near us. My clearest memory was of the fat trailer park manager driving around in her pink Thunderbird convertible, shouting at us kids in a thick Texas accent.

I drove slowly through the trailer park, stopping when I got to the old swimming pool, now empty, dirty and cracked, enclosed in a chain-link fence. This was the site of one of my scariest childhood memories.

Mom was sunbathing at one end of the pool. I was five or six, walking toward a group of older kids who were laughing and teasing each other. To get their attention, I started kicking a soda can around on the concrete, keeping my eyes on them, as I bumbled my way around the pool making as much noise as possible. Then I turned, took a step, and fell right into the deep end. Silently disappearing. Floating down through the cool blue water. At first it was thrilling, like I had stumbled into a secret world. Then my chest seized up and I flailed my arms wildly and kicked madly. I may have drowned if an old Russian woman hadn't pulled me out by my hair.

Driving through the Alhambra Trailer Park felt like passing through a weird warp in time. As if I was a little boy again, caught up in the wondrous and frightening feeling that the trailer park was a magic place, a hidden place, that most people didn't even know existed.

It was still dusk when I got back to my mother's house. I put on my jacket and a cap and took my burrito and a beer out back to enjoy the fresh air before it got dark. A sleek gray mockingbird flew down from the power line and landed on the fence, cocking its head in my direction.

I turned toward it and sheepishly admitted that I liked sitting in my mother's backyard, in the evening light—even if my mother was in the hospital. And that I liked being there alone, without Paula or Lily. Free of the stickiness of family.

The mockingbird flipped up its tail and fluttered its wings, then started chattering every which way but straight. Mocking my glorification of solitude.

A moment later a blue jay landed on the wire and aggressively hopped in the mockingbird's direction. The mockingbird shot up in the air flashing its light gray belly feathers, then dove straight down at the jay, which tumbled off the wire, regrouped, then attacked again. The mockingbird darted a few yards away and screamed something in Mexican Spanish, or Fresno Armenian, or Okie relocation drawl.

Then the cycle began all over again. Both birds dive-bombing, swooping, swooning, and swearing aggressively at each other. Until the blue jay retreated to the next yard, and the victorious mockingbird blurted out an ecstatic victory song from its tiny gray throat, claiming the yard and the last rays of sunlight for itself.

Later that night, I sat on my mother's sea-green couch and felt a story flowing through the tips of my fingers onto the keyboard and materializing on my laptop screen. It was another of the short, cerebral, fable-like pieces, I had started writing when my mother's health had, once again, taken a turn for the worse. The words popped into my head without my having to think about them, like a broadcast transmission, and once again I felt the pinprick of excitement, and I gave in to the pleasure of making things up that didn't matter.

Now, I realize how foolish those fables were. Rather than distracting myself with made-up stories, I should have used that time to talk to my mother. To learn more about her childhood in Detroit, and her older father from Scotland—whom she always spoke warmly of; and her teenage mother—whom she usually turned into a villain; and her time in Southern California with my father—who she glorified; and her long years in Fresno with my stepdad—who seemed to drain the life out of her.

Of course, my mother had tantalized me with bits and pieces of stories over the years, but she didn't like to talk about her life very much. That sort of thing was difficult for her. And the truth is that when I visited her, I wanted to be mothered, like all children, no matter how old we get.

Still, I wonder why I let myself get so distracted making up those stories, which I often spoke into my phone while driving home from Fresno. It's okay, I kept telling myself, they're nothing more than harmless distractions. Then I typed one up and printed it out. Then I typed another. And another. Pretty soon I began to feel a kind of blind infatuation for my abstract fables. I fantasized that they would bring my mother and me closer together. That I could be like Scheherazade reading her a new story every night as she lay in bed propped up on a pile of soft pillows.

I started to believe that the playful, inventive language, the metamorphosis, and constant transformation of the stories, would keep my mother curious and distracted and alive for months or even years.

The only problem was that my mother no longer had any patience for games of the imagination. She didn't like fiction. Hadn't read it for years. She said she was only interested in real things that happened to real people in real places and real times.

News and biography, in other words.

But not her biography. No, not that.

Makes sense, I guess. You need to believe in fiction before you want to talk about your own life.

At the hospital the next day, a new nurse, Isioma, broke into a large smile and shook my hand when I told her I was Georgiana's son.

You know, George, your mother is a very strong woman. I didn't notice it right away, but now I see it and I am truly impressed. You are a lucky man to have a mother like her.

Isioma's thick black hair was cut short. Subtle shades of purple-red makeup accentuated her eyelids and lips. Her entire face looked like it was smiling.

I slipped into Mom's room and was surprised to see her sitting up, her back braced by a couple of extra pillows. Her hair was freshly brushed, and, I noted with relief, she was eating. She put the orange juice down on the bedside table and greeted me.

George!

Her eyes were bright and sparkling. She looked like a different person—or rather, she looked like my mother.

It seems like Isioma's magic touch is doing you a world of good, I teased.

Oh, Izzy is great! Just the sound of that woman's voice makes me want to dance. And that's saying something. Oh, and Dr. Bellus came by early this morning. And I mean early. I had finally fallen asleep after being poked and prodded every couple of hours. Then the doctor shows up at the crack of dawn with a big smile on his face. Georgie, he said, if your numbers keep improving, we're going to have to send you home. I thought he was kidding.

Was he?

Ask Izzy, I'm not sure.

When my mother's heart first started failing, I thought Dr. Bellus would be the one to save her. I was confused. Dr. Bellus was a good doctor but not the superhero surgeon kind of good doctor. He was the maintenance man. His job was to keep my mother's failing heart failing for as long as possible.

I went to find Isioma. The nurses at the nursing station were laughing and telling stories in their green tops and stretchy pants. Reviewing charts. Quickly answering questions. Darting across the floor to get something from the files or to put something away. Their mood was upbeat, energetic, anticipatory. Isioma was chatting with another nurse. When she noticed me, she hurried over.

Oh, yes, she confirmed. Dr. Bellus was here this morning. And, yes, he said your mother is doing better. But, my friend, don't get your hopes up too much. She probably won't be packing her bags today, I am sorry. Maybe tomorrow, though. That is a possibility.

When I got back to mom's room, the bulky cream-colored phone next to the bed was ringing. I picked it up.

George? This is Janus. Janus Livingston.

For a moment, I didn't know who it was on the other end of the line. Then I recognized his voice. Soft and caring, yet wary and suspicious. Janus said that he had been calling and emailing for days.

When was she admitted? How's she feeling? Is she eating?

I adjusted the pillows behind Mom's back then handed her the phone. She held it in one hand and absentmindedly ran the fingers of her other hand through her hair.

I sat down and pulled the curtains open. White clouds drifted past the window like points of light in a kaleidoscope. Listening to my mother talk to Janus it was hard for me to believe that he and my childhood friend Steve were the same person. It felt like by changing his name Steve had not only put his past and his family behind him, but he had actually become a new person named Janus, with a different childhood, I knew nothing about.

When we were kids, Steve and I were best friends. He was the leader. I was the sidekick. We wandered through the fig orchards on the other side of West Ave, with our .22 caliber rifles, hunting rabbits and squirrels. We listened to rock and roll on the radio in the backyard. I played records for him. Steve played guitar for me. He'd taught himself an intricate finger-picking style, like Leo Kottke. His versions of songs like "King of the Road" and "Gentle on My Mind" were so good that when I think about them now, it seems like I am remembering real recordings that I used to own and listen to with my friends.

Sometimes Steve and I rode our bikes as far as the San Joaquin River. The river felt wild and vast and a little dangerous. The outer limits of where I was allowed to go. One time we found an abandoned canoe bobbing upside down in a tangle of branches. We hauled it to a sand bar, tipped it over to empty the water out, found a couple of long sticks to use as poles and floated downstream. Another time we came upon four girls on horseback. They rode up to a swimming hole, slipped off their horses, quickly undressed and jumped into the river. Their plump butts and small bouncing breasts were mesmerizing. Yet another time, we walked down to the river from the dirt road on the bluff looking for a place to camp. We took a shortcut under the railroad trestle, arching over our heads like an iron shadow, then veered off the trail to a level patch of ground. We heard a screeching owl then felt its wings beating on our necks. We panicked and ran, almost tumbling head over heels. One of our backpacks opened and cans of beans and corn bounced out and rolled down the hill with us.

Like many people, I've fantasized about moving to a new place and taking on a new identity. No longer George, but Gustaf, or Benjamin, or Jamie. But Janus? I laughed when my mother told me that Steve had changed his name. Janus? Really? Like the Roman god? Depicted with two faces, one looking toward the future and the other toward the past.

Later that afternoon, Janus showed up at my mother's hospital room with flowers, a small container of ice cream, some bowls, and plastic spoons. I hadn't seen him in years and was startled by his appearance. Barrel-chested and pot-bellied, his thick brown hair had thinned and turned gray and was pulled back in a ponytail. He gave me a quick nod and walked up to the bed.

Well look at you, Georgie! You look like a queen. They must be taking real good care of you.

Oh, Jan! I can't believe you brought ice cream. Can you do that?

It's okay, I'm a nurse, remember.

After we finished eating, Jan put the flowers on the windowsill and gave them a little water. He threw the spoons and bowls into the trashcan, closed the ice cream container, and handed it to me. Then he rushed off, explaining that he was late for his shift at another hospital.

The next morning, I stopped for coffee at the French bakery in Fig Garden Village. Before going inside, I paused to listen to an old man wearing a floppy bow tie, a bowler hat and a crazy over-sized checkered jacket, playing ragtime banjo.

He reminded me of a picture of my mother's father, wearing a straw hat and a woman's sweater, flexing his muscles, one pant leg rolled up exposing his bare calf. The proverbial shit-eating grin on his face.

I asked the woman who took my order about the banjo player. He was part of a Dixieland group that played during the lunch rush. He must have been well into his 80s and was still going strong.

I drove up Shaw and turned left on First. The trees on the edge of the hospital parking lot were in full color. Brittle golden yellow. Copper brown fading into dusty gray. Fragile dry red and burnt orange. The leaves looked like discarded Get Well cards blowing past rows of parked cars.

When I got to the main entrance, the doors opened and a woman pushing a man in a wheelchair entered ahead of me. He appeared to be in his 50s. Skin yellow and mushy. Listless hands parked on his lap. I followed slowly behind them, pausing to look at an exhibit of photographs celebrating the history of the old Saint Agnes hospital—a beautiful Spanish

Revival building topped by a red tile roof with park–like grounds, like an old European estate, with palm trees sticking up among tall pines. The photographs were moody and fascinating, taken in a time of sepia and slow exposures.

It took me a few seconds to remember that I had been born in that building. Now called Glen Agnes Elderly Housing. In the elevator, I wondered if my mother knew that the old Saint Agnes Hospital had become a nursing home—a place she might end up if things went wrong. I had to admit there was something funny about the full-circle-ness of that possibility. I imagined telling people that my mother had spent her last days in the same building, on the same floor, maybe even in the same room, where I had been born. I was still smiling when I opened the door to my mother's room. Then I froze.

Mom's head lay heavy on the stiff pillow. She looked sunken and fragile.

Water, she gasped, Thirsty! I dipped a towel into her cup and held it to her lips.

Water, more. She gasped again.

I found the control box between the mattress and the hard plastic frame and raised the back of the bed. I brought the plastic cup to her lips, and she drank a little more. She tried to talk but it came out stuttery and mixed up. Her eyes were half open and unfocused. A few seconds later she stiffened.

Nurse! Nurse! Bathroom! Nurse!

I sat with her the rest of the day. She slept a lot.

Needed little things when she was awake. A tissue. More water. The blankets adjusted. Hand cream. Another tissue. More water. I kept waiting for Izzy or Dr. Bellus to show up, but neither of them did.

I dreaded calling Paula. This time she picked up. At first, she was scared. Then she accused me of sleeping on the job, twiddling my thumbs, basically of sitting there doing nothing other than waiting for the hospital to get its dirty claws into my mother's neck. I was shaken by what she said, but I had to admit that she wasn't all wrong.

Dr. Bellus stopped by late in the afternoon. Your mother has developed a fever and probably has an infection. Not good, he admitted, but it happens.

For the next few days, Mom rarely opened her eyes and hardly spoke. Nurses came to check the machines. Orderlies brought and picked up trays of food. It turned out that Izzy had been working the night shift. One morning she stayed late to talk to me. Your mother is slipping away, George. But I won't let her slip all the way away.

I sat in the stiff beige chair next to the bed and stared at my mother's face, hoping for a sign. Her body was completely still. Only the machines told me she was alive. Then I noticed a subtle rippling under her forehead. Like an intense struggle of concentration was going on. As if she was directing all her energy to her bones, her muscles, her vital organs. Telling them to hold on, just a little longer. Promising that she'd bounce back. That it wasn't her time yet.

Dr. Bellus' reports were vague and inconclusive. Every time he had good news, bad news followed. Then just when the bad news had piled up to the point where I gave up hope, he told me something surprisingly positive.

Paula said she'd be there in a day or two, as soon as she lined up someone to watch Lily. In the meantime, we teased through the finer points of all the what ifs we could think of. We scenarioed left and right, high and low. But inevitably, no matter where we started and how much ground we covered, the conversation always ended with Paula making me swear an oath.

The moment your mother gets better you must immediately get her out of the hospital. No matter what the doctors and nurses say. There is nothing they can do to stop you. Promise me you'll do that, alright George?

One night, in the middle of all this limbo, I was sitting in my old bedroom, which Mom called her computer room, when her cheap, black, filing cabinet caught my attention. I pulled it open and started flipping through the files, reading the labels, some typed, some handwritten, looking for insight into how her mind worked, or at least how she organized things.

She had saved so many useless pieces of paper. Old bills, manuals for machines she no longer owned, advertisements for vacations she never took, recipes for food she never made and wouldn't have eaten if she did, records of employment and unemployment, records of health and illness.

I found it all very predictable, comforting even. She wasn't excessive or obsessive, and she wasn't negligent either. Then I found a file that reminded me there was another side to my mother. A file labeled, Early Life w/ Whitey, Various "journals," notes, picts.

I pulled it out and laid it on top of the desk. Inside was a stack of pages typed on sheets of thick multi-colored construction paper. The first entry was mossy-green.

Journal Kept at Tamarack Ridge, Calif.
In the High Sierras.
Oct. 22, 1956

Mr. L accompanied by Mrs. L left the Mother
Lode—Wells Fargo town of Jackson —1200 ft.—for
a Shangri La in the forests of the great Sierra Nevada
Mountain range at an elevation of around 6800 ft.
Scenery—complete with pine trees and many awe-
some sequoias and God knows how many thousands
of other species of tree and plant life. No smog here.
The first entry into this illustrious ledger being
made by the generous glow of kerosene stove
and encouraging cheers from Mr. L..... such as:
And where the hell is the toothbrush...

Needless to waste time space & energy by going into
the drab details...colorful as they are...of all the road-
blocks & obstacles that had to be overridden to achieve
this evening...as they were numerous indeed! I will do

my duty to posterity by listing the last lesson here: a
mere itch in view of all the other irritations—which was
a blow out on our way up the mountain, just a few miles
from our secluded destination. We had rented a trailer
in Laguna Beach to load most of the supplies & junk we
intended leaving in Fresno…it was bulging & threatening to burst every bump in the road and eventually wore
on the tires, espec. on the steep grade up to the cabin.

Mr. L. hit the sack this first night with a hoarse
comment on the icy sheets…my only con-
cern at the moment being that he arises with
the sun to light the goddamned fire!

The shelter we find ourselves in tonight is construct-
ed of rough logs on the exterior—quite solid tho—I
believe. The interior, although without electricity
and what is commonly recognized as comfortable
furniture, is cozy, bright, and spacious enough for two
humans. Also, there is an inside john and running,
bitterly cold, water. Unfortunately, we dragged the
hi-fi with us plus two radios… none of which will be of
much use without 'juice.' Underneath months of dust
we did find, in one corner of the living rm, a vintage
"Sonora" hand-winding phonograph. Hunting further,
we discovered a number of records among which we
chose "Indian Love Call" for the trial run. It worked.
Mr. L. Are you asleep????

The only light in the computer room came from
the small green desk lamp, which I had turned to
shine on my mother's journal pages. It felt like I too
was sitting in a rustic cabin tucked away in the dark,
reading. My mother's young, typed-up voice was

bright and lively. She came across as strong and witty, with a warm and excited curiosity. I could see why my father was attracted to her, why he wanted her by his side as they settled in for a long winter.

The next entry was typed on dark blue construction paper.

Oct. 23, 1:30 P.M.

Scream Wind, Scream! Clouds, Snow! It must have started early this AM because we awoke to a changed & chilled & transparent, white planet. Mr. L. woke to my jolly screams of child-like delight which left me when I first envisioned the scene... For as much as I know on the subject, this might be the only thing we'll see until Spring! And we came so well stocked too! Food for at least 2 or 3 weeks. Guess the other 4 months we'll have to kill some game & pick wild berries. Being the seasoned mountaineers we are, we decided to wait and buy our supplies after we became a little more settled. We KNEW it wouldn't snow for WEEKS. Our salvation! The car too, which we planned to store in Arnold, is sitting frigidly outdoors, huddled close to the cabin almost lost to view, underneath all that powder.

An unhappy event...And only the 2nd day in state too. Our phonograph gave us the old heave ho and came to a groaning, grumbling, decisive & permanent stop. It's up to the heavenly angels to sing to us now.

AND AWAY INTO THE BLIZZARD
I GO...if I can get all these clothes on before nightfall. My God—that wind!

5:40 P.M.
Bent my domestic mind & talents to baking biscuits in
the old wood stove...my first experience with the damn
stove & I underestimated the intense heat...now everything that went in so white could come out so black!

The snow hasn't stopped all day. We met a man from the
hwy. dept., while taking a walk this noon, who gleefully
informed us that if another foot falls tonight the road
would not be cleared. CAN THIS BE TRUE??

Reading these journal entries was bittersweet.
My mother had been a spirited writer, full of passion and verve. What happened to all that energy? I
glanced up at the cork bulletin board hanging next
to her computer monitor and saw one answer to that
question. A short letter she had written to the editor
of the *Fresno Bee*, extolling the overwhelmingly clear
logic of railroad consolidation. Her passion project
late in life.

Two sets of tracks run through Fresno. Southern
Pacific along the west edge of town, and the Burling-
ton Northern Santa Fe, which slashes diagonally right
through the center of Fresno. Rattling windows and
waking sleepers in a dozen neighborhoods, including
hers.

She joined a small group of activists who wanted
to consolidate both lines and force BNSF to stop running its trains through town. She went to meetings,
wrote emails, stood up in city council sessions. Her
letter to the editor was a well-crafted, sarcastic, rant.

The passion was still there, but all the warmth and humor had been squeezed out.

The next entry was typed on bright red construction paper:

Oct. 24, 1956, 11:00 P.M.

Since the weather didn't remain so ominous as expected, I made the trip into San Andreas today with Milo, owner of Tamarack Lodge & Russ Schaefer, field man for the weather Co. to purchase enough grub to last at least 6 months. It consumed the whole day & $380.00 for food stuffs plus $69 for ¼ of a steer. Seemed like a hell of an amount of food when it was being ordered, wrapped & piled on Milo's truck... will seem like even more when I begin to find storage room for it all. We left early this morn. and returned about 7 this eve. Mr. L. stayed behind to tend the fires. The PG&E crew installed the radio equipment, antenna, generator, etc. today. Mr. L has been complaining loud & clear about the gross inefficiency & negligence of this outfit (Weather Co.). They'd done the job of installing us with the least amount of effort & consideration they could safely get away with. But installed we are and I, as a party of one, am happy about it.

A few more entries followed, all typed on a rainbow of thick sheets of paper. She was enjoying herself. Both the drudgery of cabin life and writing about it. She was 25-years old. Newly married. Living a life she may have dreamed of, but never expected would be hers.

Her writing was smart and biting, opinionated and on the mark. I loved how she poked fun at my father's big plans, his grandiose convictions. How she marveled at hearing radio stations from New Orleans and Mexico on the short wave. How she loved shooting a gun in the morning and baking a cake in a wood stove in the afternoon.

She's bored. She's ecstatic. She's worried. She's blissfully sarcastic. She can't believe she's living on top of the world, above the trees, beneath shockingly vivid skies.

But even with all that energy, the journal entries peter out after only a couple of weeks. It must have been hard for her to write with another writer in that tiny cabin. A man who had to pump himself up like a leaky tire every morning.

I've come to wonder if she simply found it easier to keep her stories in her head, where there could be more richness, variation, enjoyment even—once she forgot about the page and let the words live in the air where nobody could question them.

There's a photograph from the fire-watch time that I'm particularly fond of. My mother standing in a patch of snow, smiling, wearing a black swimsuit and dark sunglasses, with a large hunting rifle slung over her shoulder.

The days at the hospital wore on and on until finally one afternoon Dr. Bellus led me into a small conference room. His pale brown hair now pressed to the side of his head looked dirty and greasy. He sat down at an oval table and gestured for me to take one of the chrome-framed chairs directly across from him.

Your mother's not responding to treatment, George.

He was hesitant. Didn't make eye contact. I stared at his wrinkled white coat and dark blue shirt.

You don't think she'll get better, this time? I asked.

His shoulders tensed. He put both hands on the table and looked down. Maybe not, he mumbled.

He raised his eyes, then quickly lowered them. He started to say something, then stopped.

He doesn't know what to say or how to act, I realized. I wanted to grab him and shake him. Don't fail me now, doctor. You should be a pro at this. You must have had this conversation hundreds of times. Turn on your real fake emotions like a priest or funeral parlor director. Memorize your lines. Play your part.

A few seconds later, he straightened up in his chair and said that he was sorry. Then he asked if I had a place for her to go. He paused, took a short breath, then added, tentatively, I think it's time to consider hospice.

I waited for him to say something more, to try to console me. When he didn't, I hurried out of the room without looking at him, and headed for a small courtyard I remembered seeing, near the cafeteria.

I passed a set of large, glossy photographs of joyful oversized fruits and vegetables, cut open and arranged in semi-abstract patterns. *Cheer up, people!* The fruit shouted. *Think healthy thoughts!* I wanted to rip the photographs off the walls.

I glared at the overweight and miserable people inside the cafeteria. I blamed Dr. Bellus for the photos of happy fruits and vegetables. And for the unhealthy cafeteria people. And for the song, "This is the End," which I hadn't heard, or thought of, for years, suddenly blasting in my head. And for Jim Morrison's funereal baritone.

As I sat on a stone bench in the sheltered courtyard, with a saint fountain bubbling next to me, staring blankly at a bright red maple, images of Día de los Muertos altars from earlier that month flooded into my mind. Each altar appeared lovely and touching, decorated with photographs of the deceased and bright orange marigolds, piles of fruit and plates of sweets and arrangements of sugar skulls.

Paula lingered at each one, but I hurried past them all, put off by the glitz. Until I saw an altar set away from the main path, consisting of a simple white skeleton reclining on a wooden pew under a tree. A woman wrapped in a red velvet blanket, her head propped up on a bony arm, two candles illuminating her face.

The stark serenity of the altar drew me in. No flowers, no skulls, no image of the deceased, only a solitary peaceful figure stretched out on an old pew resting under a tree—and the words, *Sacred Sleep*, scrawled in luminescent chalk behind her.

The sounds of the fountain brought the hospital back into focus. Reminding me of all the futile machines, with their harsh blips and beeps, surrounding my mother in her mechanical bed. It felt like every-thing in the hospital was designed to squeeze the last few ounces of life out of her. Why? I wondered. For what?

Then, I had a vision of Isioma sweeping into my mother's room and ordering everything taken away. I saw her gently lift my mother out of bed and put her in my arms. A carpet was rolled out on the floor, candles lit, a feather bed brought in with silk sheets. I saw myself getting into bed with my mother and lying there with her, listening to Isioma sing until we both fell asleep.

It was dark when I pulled into the driveway later that night, unlocked the back door, and flipped on the kitchen light. While the cats were eating, I sat down at the table and called Paula. Once again, she didn't pick up. I knew she wasn't ignoring me. She had just forgotten her phone in the bathroom, or maybe in the car. Still, it was frustrating.

I left her a message: Call me as soon as you get this. It's important. Up until then, I had been glad that Paula hadn't come to Fresno. We usually butt heads and can't agree on what to do or when to do it. But now, for the first time, I really wished she was there with me. I was starting to lose it. I needed help.

I got up from the table and squatted in front of the sink. I opened the cabinet door and fished around behind the blue bucket containing old cleaning sup-plies until I felt my mother's oversized plastic bottle of Save Mart scotch. I poured myself a glass and took my drink into the living room.

After my mother had been rushed to the hospital the first three or four times, then released healthier a week or two later, I got used to it. I came to see her time in the hospital as necessary down time, time for her to recuperate, to rejuvenate. I started to believe that the cycle would keep repeating itself, forever. Of course, I knew that the spinning top always slows down, starts to wobble, and topples over. But that didn't stop me from believing in magic. The magic of closing my eyes, the magic of staying busy, the magic of not asking too many painful questions.

But hospice is hospice, I reminded myself, it doesn't matter if your eyes are open or closed. It's emergency time, and I'm all alone in my mother's house, fumbling and mumbling my way to the couch.

Paula! I called out, help!

I put a CD in the player and sat down on the couch. Bill Evans, Scott LaFaro and Paul Motian, *Live at the Village Vanguard*. They sounded terrible. Distracted. Bored. Like they were waiting for the CD to end so they could slip back into the land of the dead where they no longer had to listen to their past selves.

I was just about to turn off the music when something changed. Bill Evans discovered yet another way into a tune he'd played a thousand times. The piano became more introspective, more resonant. Melody lines like incantations twined their way into the pulse of the bass, the subtle plot shifts of the drums.

I thought about what Dr. Bellus had said. Hospice meant my mother had maybe six months to live. Possibly more. She had always been a strong woman. She could beat the odds and return home with a clear mind and settled heart. It was possible, even likely, I reassured myself.

I tried calling Paula again. Then I closed my eyes and laid my head against the back of the couch. Three loud blasts from a passing train rattled the windows. The walls of the house started to vibrate. The ceiling vaporized. A strong breeze danced across the floor and the floor embraced it and vanished. Then it was just me, the sturdy couch, the hard bare ground. A fire sputtering at my feet.

The neighbor's houses retreated toward the horizon. Fresno faded as well. All its mean ugliness whipped up and carried away by the stiff night wind.

Driving up Herndon the next morning, the air smelled like a farmer on the outskirts of town had buried a huge pile of smoldering leaves that were hot and smoky.

Paula finally called back, just as I was pulling into the hospital parking lot. I told her what Dr. Bellus had said about hospice. At first, she took it calmly. As if she had expected the news. Then she started blaming.

She blamed the doctor. The nurses. Me. You waited too long, George! You let your mother sit in the hospital getting sicker and sicker! I should have been there. I would have gotten her out, before it was too late.

After we hung up, I leaned my head on the steering wheel and cried, hard, for the first time that week.

I got out of the car and walked up the hill to the hospital. I got to my mother's room and was relieved to find her sleeping. There was an open orange juice box, a milk container, and a half-finished coffee cup on the plastic tray.

I sat down on the chair next to the bed and she immediately woke up. She asked if I had fed her cats. She asked if she had any mail. She said she wanted something from home to make her feel more comfortable. A blanket or warm sweater.

Isioma came in to check my mother's fluid intake. She gave me a quick glance that felt like an apology. When she was gone, Mom asked about her cats again. And whether I could get her some crackers or yogurt. Then she mentioned Dr. Bellus and looked away.

I squeezed her hand. It's okay, Mom. I know. I'm sorry.

She looked up at me, her eyes watery, her lips trembling.

Dr. Bellus told me he doesn't think you have much more time.

She jerked her hand out of mine. That's ridiculous! He doesn't know what he's talking about! There are too many things I still need to do.

Of course, it was her denial talking. But I didn't care. I loved her denial. I wanted it to last forever.

As the day wore on, my anger simmered over to a boil. The clockwork efficiency, which made sense when the goal was to stabilize my mother and get her home, felt like the worst kind of hypocrisy. Something else was called for. Flowers instead of mushy potatoes. Singers instead of nurses carrying Dixie cups full of pills. You can't just tell someone they're going to die, and soon, and then pretend like nothing has changed.

It took a couple more days for all the arrangements to be made. The hospital agreed to release my mother. The insurance company agreed to pay to transport her to Berkeley. Paula got everything lined up with the hospice agency. A hospital bed and bedside commode and other supplies had been delivered. Morphine was on the shelf.

When I returned to my mother's room in the afternoon, Isioma was sitting next to the bed, with her hand on my mother's arm.

George, your mother is feeling much better, this would be a good time for you to talk to her.

Mom's eyes were distant and cloudy, but they were open. Do you remember when we talked about you coming home with us after you get out of the hospital, rather than staying in Fresno? She turned her head in my direction but didn't say anything. What do you think about that now? She blinked. Paula and I think it's better if you come home with us, okay?

Once she fell asleep again, I walked to the waiting room around the corner and called Paula. She picked up and did her best to console me. Your mom will be much more comfortable with us, she promised. It'll be way better than being alone in her house with a nurse.

When I got off the phone, I felt like we had made the right decision. My mother would finally get out of Fresno. She would live close to the ocean again, like she always said she wanted to, where the moist air smelled of salt and other shores.

I visited my mother's hospital room one more time the next morning. We had pretty much the same conversation as the day before. She said she wanted to come to Berkeley. But I wasn't sure whether she understood that meant she probably would never see her house in Fresno again. I told her the ambulance would be there after lunch, that Izzy would help her get ready. I was going to leave earlier so that I could be home when she got there.

Mom panicked and sat up in bed and grabbed my hand. Don't leave me alone! I held her hand for a few moments, then kissed her cheek and told her that I loved her.

When I pulled out of the hospital parking lot, I felt shaky and lightheaded. I turned left on Herndon, got on Highway 99 just before the San Joaquin River, and set the cruise control.

All the arrangements we had made and the reasons for making them spun around and around in my head. My gut tightened and my certainty faded. Maybe it's a mistake moving Mom to Berkeley? Maybe I should turn around and tell the ambulance driver to take her back to Brooks Ave?

I kept driving, on emotional and psychological autopilot, dangerously unaware of anything around me. When I snapped out of my delirium, I realized I had gotten off the freeway. But instead of turning around and heading back to Fresno, I was driving down a country road surrounded by almond trees.

The road dead-ended at what appeared to be an abandoned baseball field. I parked, got out of the car, and wandered into the knee-high weeds and wild grasses. A flock of starlings zig-zagged across the sky. I stumbled around for a few minutes until I found what was left of the pitcher's mound.

I remembered the time I took my mother to the 2002 World Series in San Francisco. Game 4. Giants and Angels. She loved it. The high-energy crowd followed every nuance of the game like a collective body. Sighing, cheering, jumping out of their seats at exactly the same moment. And my mother was right there with them. Swept up in the passion of the game.

The World Series was everything she hoped it would be. Her father had taken her to Tiger Stadium in Detroit when she was a little girl. Her elderly father, with his thin white hair, fat nose and joyful eyes, had taken her to Tiger Stadium. And now, late in life, her son had taken her to the World Series in San Francisco.

Without thinking, I picked up a rock and hurled it at the backstop. My grandfather, George Edwin Allen, stood at the plate. He intentionally swung late. Strike three. Take a seat, meat. Someone yelled from the bleachers. Next up was my uncle, Edward Delano Allen. I threw another rock as hard as I could. He let loose with all he had and sent it flying over the left field fence.

I was elated. Somehow my family had found me in that abandoned municipal baseball field. Great aunts and uncles, distant cousins, and great-great grandparents. They swarmed around me, and I was overwhelmed by their warmth and love.

Someone said, why'd you throw inside, dumb-shit? Everyone knows Eddie clobbers anything inside. It was Grandfather George. His joyful old face; thin, shaggy, white hair; and twinkling brown eyes, were right in front of me. He placed his hand on my shoulder and guided me away from the rest of the family.

Hey there, George. What's shaking?

His voice was low and resonant, with a carefree seriousness to it. My mind spiraled. My heartbeat plummeted. My legs felt heavy. I stuck out my hand and stammered, nice to finally meet you, grandpa.

Good joke! He chuckled. Then he said, in a much more serious tone, now look, son, this is no time for small talk. You need to get home, right now. Your mother needs you.

I sat down on the dugout bench, shivering and alone. The air was acrid. A vector of geese rose from fallow fields. The cars rushing along the freeway a mile or two away canceled each other out.

Mom arrived at our house a few hours later, in a beat-up van, half-conscious. They carried her inside on a stretcher and lifted her onto the hospital bed in Paula's office.

Days passed and Mom didn't seem aware of anything around her. The fact that she was with us in Berkeley, in a room overlooking our garden, was meaningless. As were the burning candles and classical music we left playing for her.

One afternoon she recovered enough to sit up. Her room was full of autumn sunlight and cut flowers. She opened her eyes. But didn't say a word.

Less than a week later, I fell asleep at the foot of her bed like a loyal dog.

Next morning, she was gone.

And I felt as confused and anxious as any dog would feel when his master has left,

and he knows she is never coming back again.

Chapter Three

MEN WILL BE MEN

[mom]

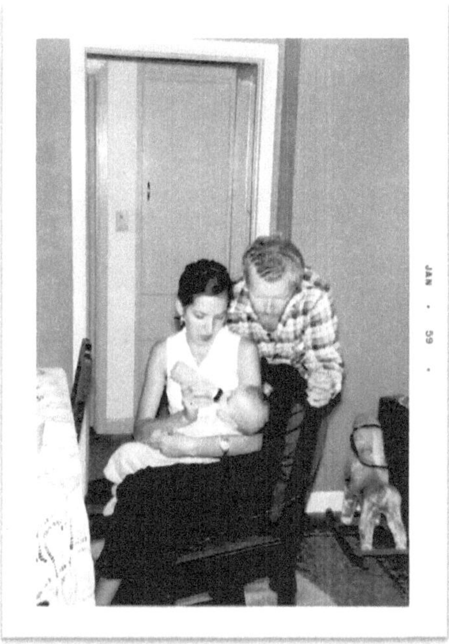

Details are different when you're dead. Sometimes they float around in space, drifting every which way, becoming isolated from their memories, fading into ever more insubstantial shadows. Then again, even the slightest memory has gravitational pull. Attracting forgotten bits of experience into new configurations—not all of them true—transfixing and overwhelming in their spectacle.

What I mean is, every story becomes a labyrinth. Every memory a wormhole.

When I was alive, it was easy to pass judgment and have preferences.

To think it mattered if someone was short or tall.

Or if someone drank whisky and not apple juice.

Or played golf and not checkers.

Or read poetry and not mysteries.

Of course, it all matters, or can, depending on the kind of life you want to live.

But now that I'm dead, I embrace all the opposites, the contradictions, the variations that life screams into the darkness.

I remember the name Noreen. And a place called Arcadia Lumber, east of Los Angeles. I remember that Noreen was the best thing about working at Arcadia Lumber when I was there in the mid 1950s.

What else?

She was the bookkeeper. I was just the front counter girl. That didn't matter, we hit it off right away. Still, I wasn't sure how long I'd last at the lumber company. The incessant screaming of the saws, the swirling wood dust, the jittery floors from the comings and goings of the guys in their heavy boots, got on my nerves.

I remember that before I got the job at the lumber company, I worked in the hushed atmosphere of Uncle Bill's big house in Pasadena. And before that, there was the peacefulness of the San Antonio Public Library. My first job after leaving Detroit.

San Antonio was a real cow town, just like I had dreamed of.

Horses. Cowboys. The hot dry Texas landscape.

Pure bliss for a Michigander girl like me.

Then I got a call from Uncle Bill. Would I come out to California to help him take care of his wife, Maxine? She had once been a beautiful actress and singer, but now had cancer.

Come to California? I repeated, trying not to sound too excited. I loved the cowboy life in San Antonio, but I loved the idea of California even more.

When I got to Pasadena, the joke was on me. Maxine was old and sick. Her shiny blond hair had thinned. Her pale green eyes had turned dull gray. She was emaciated and hardly spoke. My job was to keep her company, and to get her dressed, put a little makeup and lipstick on her face, and brush her hair as many times a day as she'd let me. I didn't see much of Uncle Bill and even less of Los Angeles.

As Maxine got sicker, I remember sitting next to her bed and patting her forehead with a damp washcloth. I remember giving her small sips of water from a delicate blue and white teacup. She became so thin and fragile that I had a hard time looking at her. My eyes felt dangerous. Like they could break one of her bones without my ever knowing it.

At least Maxine's room was lovely. A large, hypnotically beautiful, Persian carpet lay on the floor next to the bed, and small oil paintings hung on the wall like in a museum, with fancy frames and labels.

In one painting two pigeons sat on a hard brown rock looking at an otherworldly bloom of purple and blue light filling the sky over the ocean. I must have spent hours looking at that painting, waiting for Maxine to wake up and need something, wishing that the painting had the power to lift me out of that house, to transport me across the black-blue water, and leave me on the rock next to those peaceful birds.

As the days stretched into weeks and months, I started to worry. Maxine might last a long time. I could get old sitting next to her bed, with just me, myself, and I for company.

When Maxine finally died, Uncle Bill's fancy life no longer had any room for me. I became depressed and lonely. If I hadn't gotten the job at Arcadia Lumber, I probably would have left California. Maybe for good.

Noreen and I liked to take our breaks together. If the weather was good, we'd stand outside and have a smoke, and chat about what was going on in our lives. It was nice having a friend at work—and having a job that wasn't so emotionally taxing.

What do you like to do for fun? Noreen asked one afternoon.

I don't know. Normal things, I guess.

Want to go to Santa Anita with me after work? The drinks are cheap, and the horses are gorgeous.

She was right. Just being around the horses was a thrill. After that, I went to the track as often as I could. That's where I met George's dad, Whitey. He walked right up to us in the stands and asked if he could get us something to drink.

Who are you to butt your head into our wonderful afternoon? I barked at him.

Don't get excited, he laughed, flashing a great big insecure smile, I'm just the janitor...here to sweep you off your feet.

That's what he did, too. He wasn't a particularly good-looking man. No taller than me, if you didn't count the three or four inches of kinky blond hair shooting out of his head in every direction. His hair was more white than blond, which is where he got his nickname. He was thin as a post with pale skin that burned quickly in the sun. He had small blue eyes, thin lips and a weak chin. But he was older, which was a good thing in my book. And he could talk like nobody I had ever met.

I told Noreen that Whitey could talk a fisherman out of his bait, a drunk out of his bottle, and a queen out of her crown. She rolled her eyes. Then I told her he had talked me out of my dress and pantyhose on our third date. That surprised her. Noreen thought I was a good ex-Catholic girl who didn't like to mess around just for the fun of it.

Slow it down with this guy, Noreen tried to warn me. I think you're in way over your head. But there was no slowing down with Whitey. He was either running full steam ahead or screeching to a stop.

One day at work, after I closed out the cash register and was cleaning up the counter, sticking new business cards in the little plastic holder, and putting away the pins and paperclips and scraps of paper and other clutter, Doug came up from behind and grabbed me around the waist.

He slid his hands over my hips and onto my stomach. You sure smell sweet, darling. Sweet as the roses I got for you in my office. Come on baby, he growled, throwing his arm over my shoulder, and pushing me toward his door.

I don't know what would have happened if Whitey hadn't stuck his head in the office right at that moment. When he saw Doug pawing me, he jumped over the counter and rushed at him with the intent to kill flashing in his eyes. Doug let go and stumbled back a few steps bracing for a fight. But Whitey just grabbed my arm and marched me out of the office.

Who was that? Whitey demanded, once we were sitting in his car.

His name is Doug. I stammered.

Well, tell little Dougie that if he ever does something like that again, I'm going to send him on a one-way trip to the moon.

We pulled out of the parking lot onto Huntington Drive, then made our way slowly through town before getting on the freeway to Laguna Beach, where Whitey lived in a trailer park a block or two from the beach.

You know, men wouldn't treat you like that if you were a married woman, Whitey joked.

Then that would be your job, right? I ribbed him.

Come on, we get along great, right? You can't deny it. Why don't we drive to Las Vegas right now and get hitched? What do you say?

I say you're already doing a fine job of protecting me.

Whitey first asked me to marry him about a month after we met, and he didn't stop. I don't want to live in your little tuna can trailer, I told him. That's fine for you, but I like to have real walls around me and a real floor under my feet. That's what I said, but secretly I liked the idea of living with Whitey on the sandy strip of land where his trailer was parked, where you could hear the waves breaking in bed, and where it was possible to believe that the rest of America didn't exist.

If Whitey had been as dependable as the waves I would have said yes in a heartbeat. I was 24 years old, after all. A good age to get married. But he had just gotten out of prison, and I thought that I could still see the crazy in his eyes.

He swore that it was the guy he was with who had the gun and that he was just the driver. And that nobody got hurt, and that he only had to do 4 years out of 12 because of good behavior, and that he started writing in prison, and that writing was his life, no more senseless criminal behavior for him, and that there's only one thing missing for him now, and that one thing is what you see every day when you look in the mirror, Georgie.

The problem with talkers like Whitey is that it's hard to tell if they mean what they say, or if they're just overly enamored with whatever comes out of their mouths. I figured I'd give it some time. To see if he was serious.

Later that week, after work, Noreen and I went to a bar she liked. A cinder block bunker stuck between a Chinese restaurant and a beauty parlor. I grabbed a table while she ordered martinis. The decor was no decor. The lighting was a dim everlasting twilight. The music was a mix of low-key crooners and jazzy ballads.

When I told Noreen what happened with Doug, she said, I hate to inform you of this, Georgie, but all the guys at Arcadia Lumber are creeps. Doug, Mikey, Sam, Bill, even the owner Al if he gets a few drinks in him. They're all jerks. You have to have a zero-flirting policy. Not even the slightest smile. Or they'll be all over you, understand? Every single one of them has a hamster brain and a wind-up dick.

And, she continued, switching to her big sister voice, try not to be too impressed that Whitey came to your rescue. Any guy would have done that. Whitey threatened Doug and Doug backed down. If Doug had challenged Whitey, then Whitey would have laid off. You get it?

I wasn't so sure Noreen was right. If Doug hadn't backed down, I bet Whitey would have been on him like a pit bull. It wouldn't have mattered that Doug was bigger and taller. Whitey would have been at his neck with his jaws locked and that would have been that for Dougie.

The music changed to Frank Sinatra singing *I've Got You Under My Skin*. Cole Porter's lovely tune. How could Frank be so in control and so nonchalant at the same time? His voice was the very essence of suave. Frank's the kind of man I want, I quipped to Noreen. Cool, sophisticated, and tough when it really matters. Problem is, there just aren't enough Sinatra-types to go around.

Two martinis later Noreen told me that she and my little brother Eddie had gone to the track together. Eddie came out to California a few years before me, to get away from a wife and a kid in Georgia.

Eddie? Really, Noreen?

Yea, and I won $750.

I'm thrilled you won so much money and I know Eddie is as cute as an Italian race car driver, but he doesn't exactly treat women very well either.

Oh, is that a fact?

I'm afraid it is.

So, he's not a gentleman like Whitey?

No, he's not.

Don't tell me you're getting serious about this guy, Georgie?

What if I am?

I think you need to get away from him for a while. He's messing with your head. I'll tell you what, let me take you to this little desert resort I know next weekend. My treat. It's nothing fancy, but there's a swimming pool, a bar and a café. It'll be a blast.

I remember that first morning at the resort. I woke up early. Noreen was still sleeping, and I didn't feel like staring at the ceiling, so I got dressed and slipped outside. I walked to the edge of the parking lot and looked across at the emptiness on the other side of the road. It was so quiet I started to worry that something bad had happened to my hearing. Burst eardrums or worse. I took a couple of steps dragging my feet, checking if I had suddenly gone deaf. Then I noticed the jittery electric Food and Lodging sign buzzing behind me and knew that I was fine.

The desert looked like a dehydrated ocean from the distant past. Dead. Still. Quiet. Everything on the other side of the highway looked like a bone yard. The rocks, the cactus, the sand, even the deeply scarred hills and feathery dunes. I was drawn in their direction but scared to walk into the desert by myself. That may have been the first time I seriously considered saying yes to Whitey's proposal.

I turned around and crossed the parking lot and headed to the coffee shop. Much to my relief, Noreen was sitting in a booth holding a brown mug between her hands.

I thought you ran off with a truck driver and left me here all alone, she sighed.

I might have if I could have found one. It's so dead out there I thought someone had stolen my pulse!

Oh, Georgie don't start with your exaggerating so early in the morning. You'll wear me out.

Noreen thought I was a fluttery moth, an excitable puppy. But I just liked to throw my feelings around like paint. To see what looked good and what didn't.

The resort was a sprawly place next to the highway. A huge imposition of alien grass on desert austerity. Bungalow, bungalow, grass. Bungalow, grass, grass. And even more glaringly green grass.

Our little room with two wooden beds and red frilly cowboy curtains was a short walk to the swimming pool, which is where we headed in the afternoon.

I wore a black one piece. Simple and sexy. The water felt amazing. Having grown up in Detroit, it was hard for me to believe that I was swimming outside in February. Noreen sat on her lounger wrapped in a fuzzy white robe holding the newspaper to her chest like she was about to start reading. I had to nag her for fifteen minutes straight before she finally stood up and dropped her robe in a heap on the grass and got into the pool with me.

Noreen may have been short and a little round, but she was cute as a button in her bathing suit. When she floated on her back with her dark shoulder-length hair fanning out around her head and her flowery swimsuit pointing up at the sky, it reminded me of lily pads.

After swimming we sat in the grassy shade with our cigarettes and magazines. Kids were everywhere. Boys playing catch on the grass. Girls jumping rope and riding bikes. Older kids shouting as they jumped into the pool, gripping their knees to see who could splash the most people with the biggest cannon ball.

Want children? I asked Noreen.

Sure, don't you?

Maybe.

What's your ex-con boyfriend say about that?

Whitey says he wants kids, but his thoughts are so jumbled on the subject I don't take him seriously. He says he wants kids, and he wants to write books, and he wants to live a simple life, and he doesn't want me to work so much, and he thinks we can do all of that and still live in Southern California.

Good luck, Noreen scoffed.

At the far end of the lawn, a grove of date palms swayed gently back and forth, like giant hula dancers with the smallest hips imaginable. We gathered up our stuff and walked toward the trees. A moment later we were standing in their thick shade and lovely, filtered light. I looked up—amazed there could be so many shades of green. Cool swirling breezes tickled my bare legs. Little canals of water gently burbled in long straight lines, soaking the roots of the palms.

Where am I? I muttered.

Paradise, Noreen started to answer. Then stopped. An old man with a droopy mustache, huddled over a long-handled hoe, had started singing in an unfamiliar language. Sonorous and clear like a deep-hearted bell. His voice gave me goosebumps.

Hey! Noreen shouted at him. Where are we?

The old man shrugged. A small white dog darted away behind him.

I turned in a slow circle, eyes wide, hands clasped, mesmerized. I wouldn't need Whitey, or any other man, to take care of me if I could live in a place like this. I kept slowly turning around, trying to find the exact right spot. There! I shrieked. That's where I want to build my house. Right in the center of the date grove, where the shadows are the darkest green and two small canals run side by side. My house on stilts. With water bubbling beneath the floor; large, shaded windows; bamboo walls; high ceilings; Persian carpets and oil paintings of desert landscapes; a princess bed with silk netting; low slung sofas covered in bright fabric in front of a picture window; and bare-chested men waiting on me hand and foot.

We stepped out of the grove, into a dusty field turned into a parking lot. We shaded our eyes, and looked around. Cars and trucks steadily rolled up the road searching for parking places. Groups of friends and families carrying ice chests and picnic baskets walked down a dirt path. A lot of them were Mexican. There were some Blacks and Asians and a few white people too. We headed toward a set of doors in the high arched wall of a stadium and got in line behind two men wearing summer suits.

Hello ladies! The short and thin one sputtered like a barker at a county fair.

LAY-DEES!

He said again looking right at me.

I ignored him with a smile.

What's going on here? Noreen asked the tall guy in a baggy light-blue suit. A bullfight?

More like a bullfight between a baseball and a bat, the tall guy informed her. Sounding like one of the sports announcers I remembered hearing on the radio when I was a girl. Knuckleball Charlie versus the Mexican Rocket. He clarified. Should be quite a match-up.

The stadium may have looked like a fortress on the outside, but inside it had wobbly wooden stairs and uneven rows of beaten-up seats. We walked past a couple of men arguing about something. We passed a large Mexican family with a feast laid out on their laps. We followed Tall Guy to the reserved seats right behind home plate. Heatwaves shimmered over the immense outfield. Teenage boys ran up and down the stairs hawking soda, candy, and hot dogs.

Noreen took the seat next to Shorty, straightening her white beach dress before sitting down, then tilting her hat to block the sun. I took the seat between her and Tall Guy, adjusting my yellow scarf to cover my head. Then I dug around in my purse until I found my burgundy sunglasses.

This year's Miss California is ready for anything now! I smirked to myself.

Ever been to a ballgame? Tall Guy asked, once I got settled.

No, I lied, but my fiancé says he's going to take me to a big league game after we're married.

Fiancé? Tall Guy repeated incredulously, brushing my shoulder with his hand as he stood up to take off his jacket.

Noreen jabbed me in the arm and whispered, fiancé? Why did you say that?

I just wanted to hear how it sounded.

And?

Not as good as I thought.

Wait, Noreen said, nudging me again, we've got to watch it with these guys. Give me a sign if you want to take off.

Tall Guy sat back down and started telling me about the game. It's the Mexicans versus the Americans, he explained. And, by the way, the Mexicans are pretty damn good. The American pitcher is Knuckleball Charlie. He's called that because he throws these slow silly pitches that almost no one can hit. He's entertaining, but don't be fooled, he's a great pitcher and a real student of the game.

I wasn't sure what he meant, but I turned and watched as the players ran onto the field. Knuckleball waited until everyone else was out, then he lumbered onto the grass and stopped like he was unsure about where to go. He sniffed the air and turned slowly in a circle before ambling toward the mound.

Knuckleball Charlie was a tall man with light-brown skin and short-cropped hair, a scruffy goatee, and hands so big the baseball looked like a robin's egg in his glove. He raised his hands to his chest, spat a few times, stared at the batter, and just stood there like a statue for what felt like ages.

When he finally got around to throwing the ball it floated out of his hand like a butterfly, fluttering left to sample the air for a hint of roses, dipping right to check for a whiff of daisies, doing a few joyful loop-de-loops before crossing the plate. The Mexicans were mystified.

While Tall Guy explained the events unfolding on the field to me, I could see Noreen making a quick study of the game of baseball. She noted the distance to the home-run fences, the number of swings that never touched the ball, the amount of time the players spent standing around without anything to do.

This game is hopeless, Georgie, she concluded. We should stick with the horse races. At least there's some action. Besides, Shorty here keeps trying to put his arm around my shoulder. And the way Tall Guy is gawking at you I don't think he believes you're getting married anytime soon.

She was right about baseball, but I didn't mind. The smell of the grass, the cigarettes, and the hot dogs, the sounds of people chatting while the game played out in front of them, the waves of excitement, sometimes barely more than a whisper, other times loud as a thunderstorm, reminded me of when my dad took me to see the Tigers play in Detroit. That was when I realized that I didn't need to understand a thing about baseball to enjoy the game.

Thinking about my dad and the Tigers leads me back to when George took me to the World Series. I was still a relatively healthy woman at that point, but I was al-

ready getting morbid. While George held my arm and gestured toward the lovely swath of green, I imagined the field was a graveyard and wondered how many people could fit in the ground there.

Everyone, I figured. All those Giants fans.

Forcing the gophers to find a new home. Or maybe bodies attract gophers? I don't know.

But I got cheerful once the game got underway. I had to. George had spent a lot of money for the tickets.

Besides, we were surrounded by life magnified a thousand times.

Big Life.

Beaming Life.

Bellowing Life.

It didn't take long before I was one with the masses, cheering like a madwoman.

But I wasn't just cheering the game. I was cheering everything I could see, taste, smell and feel, because George and Paula were about to have a baby.

When it was the American's turn to bat, The Mexican Rocket marched to the mound with his arms frozen at his sides like a gunfighter in the movies. The kind with a matchstick clenched between his teeth. He wore a red and black bandanna tied around his neck and had a bright purple dahlia tattooed on his forearm, which flashed in the sun when he pitched. He did some kind of whiplash move with his body, then stood there with both knees bent and his arms hanging limply at his side like he had just drawn and holstered a pistol. I heard what sounded like a shot being fired, but never saw the ball leave his hand.

Noreen didn't have a clue about baseball, but she was right about Tall Guy. His know-it-all attitude and wandering hands were starting to bother me. After a few more innings, I told him that Noreen and I were going to the ladies room and that we'd be right back.

We slowly made our way down the aisle. Then we walked up the stairs and through a tunnel into the long, curved hallway lined with concession stands. I took off my sunglasses and waited for my eyes to adjust.

Noreen grabbed my arm. Now hold on, Georgie, I think we need to talk about Whitey.

Really? I answered, shifting my attention to a concession stand a few yards away, where an old man with a permanent squint was serving beers to the thirsty people in line.

Noreen and I had been on a few dates together since I'd been working at Arcadia Lumber. I knew she liked to have fun. But I also knew she treated every man as Maybe-THE-man. I mean, she created a list of pros and cons for each and every guy she dated. I didn't work that way. I figured I would know the right man when I met him. No detailed analysis necessary.

We carried our beers over to a small table. A patch of sunlight struck the concrete wall next to our legs. The sounds of the game quieted down. Noreen looked up at me and said, Georgie, I'm going to be blunt. Whitey is not the guy for you. One, he's too old. Two, he's a con man. And three, he just got out of prison.

I get it, I said. You're welcome to your opinion. But the truth is, I happen to like older men. And what you call being a con man, I call having the gift of gab. And yes, he was in prison, but he wrote a novel there and got it published by a New York publisher. I call that putting your mind to something and getting it done. I call that beating the odds.

Noreen sipped her beer and shook her head. I give up, Georgie. At least he's not boring, I'll give you that. She took another sip of her beer, then asked, so, how did you like his book?

I'm not sure, I haven't finished it.

All these months and you haven't finished his book? That's not good, Georgie. That book is what's going to tell you what kind of guy he really is. You never know. Maybe his detective cracks in the end and murders his wife or something. Do me a favor and promise that you won't commit to this guy before you've finished reading his book. Okay?

Alright, Noreen, I promise I'll finish reading his book as soon as I get home. And when you're done with your beer, let's get out of here. I've had enough of our two friends.

We slipped out of the stadium and made our way back through the date grove to the motel, leaving Tall Guy and Shorty to figure things out.

The next morning we packed up and left the resort, after eating breakfast in the cafe. I was glad Noreen was driving. We listened to the radio and hardly said anything the whole way home. I stared at the road and marveled at all the twists and turns my life had taken recently.

My father had died the previous year.

My mother had married an old shoe salesman and moved to Georgia.

I had worked at a library in Texas.

And for a movie star in Pasadena.

And now I was dating a writer with sizzling blue eyes.

Yes, leaving Detroit was the best thing I had ever done.

As we got closer to LA, and the traffic began to back up, Noreen and I started talking again. We gossiped about the lumber company. We made plans for just the two of us to go to the track. She said it had been a great weekend, but a frustrating one. Why do men have to be such jerks?

Oh Noreen, you know how it is, men will always be men. I had a really nice time. Thank you.

Noreen parked a few houses down, then we crossed the neighbor's lawn to get to my front door. I knew something was off the moment I stepped inside. The red and pink hothouse roses I'd left on the kitchen table were gone. So was the Santa Anita race poster I had tacked to the wall. All my books were gone. My records and record player. Even the damn bottle of wine I had promised Noreen was gone.

In a panic she grabbed my arm, maybe somebody's still in the apartment, she gasped. I shook her off and looked around the living room. I rushed into my bedroom and flipped on the light. The closet door was open, and my clothes were gone. The dresser drawers were half open and empty. I walked over and picked up a note. I crumpled it up and threw it on the floor.

God Damn it Noreen, were you in on this? Did Whitey tell you to get me out of town for the weekend?

What are you talking about, Georgie?

Whitey came and got all my stuff when we were away. I'm going to kill that son of a bitch!

Noreen sat at the tiny table in the kitchen and kept her head down.

I paced back and forth for a few minutes.

I'm sorry, I had no idea that he was going to do that, Georgie. I swear it's not the reason I took you to the desert.

Okay, okay, I believe you. But I need to get out of here. Right now!

Want to go to my place?

No, Whitey's. I want him to see how mad I am.

I steamed out of the apartment, not even bothering to lock the front door, and jumped into Noreen's car. On the freeway to Laguna Beach, I told Noreen she had been right. Whitey's a bully. Just like the other guys. All they ever think about is knocking you down and dragging you off by the hair.

Whitey's trailer park was tucked between Highway 1 and a strip of shops that never seemed to have regular hours. I heard waves crashing when I opened the car door.

Are you sure you don't want me to come in? Noreen pleaded.

No, If I end up killing the bastard, I don't want you to be a witness.

I burst into Whitey's trailer and almost knocked over a table he had setup in the middle of the living room, with a turquoise bedspread for a tablecloth and a couple of long tapered candles dripping green wax onto empty wine bottles. Whitey was standing on the other side of the table, in the kitchen doorway, with my roses in his hand, beaming. Hey Baby, don't hate me. I just can't live without you! You get that, right?

I pushed past the table and attacked him with every muscle in my body. Shouting and wildly throwing punches. He took a few steps back then smothered me in his arms. I tried to knee him in the balls, but he pulled me tightly into his body. That's when I saw my little brother Eddie hiding in the kitchen.

You! You helped him do this! God Damn you, Eddie! Why do you always have to be such a shit?

Eddie smiled his little boy smile and buried his hands in his pockets, before disappearing into the shadows.

I've told George this story many times over the years. It happened just like this, and it didn't. Whitey and Eddie really did move all my things out of my apartment and into his trailer.

I was mad but I was also intrigued. I thought, he must really love me to do something like that. When I should have thought, he's an unbalanced, unpredictable, potentially deranged human being.

Of course, I could have moved back into my apartment. But I stayed. And we did get married. And it was both as good as I had hoped and as bad as I had feared.

We bought a vacation trailer and traveled around the country. We spent a summer on fire watch on Tamarack Ridge. We lived in San Francisco and near the beach in LA. We knew writers and artists and musicians. Whitey even published his second novel.

But Whitey wasn't comfortable being a family man with a steady job. He always needed a hustle. Even when he didn't. George knows all of that, better than almost anyone.

I also told George that Whitely hit me a few times and that I was going to divorce him if he hadn't died first. What I didn't tell him was that I wanted to leave Whitey to save his life. He was a good man and a good dad and a good writer, but he was a terrible husband-writer-dad. He couldn't do it all. Not even close. Any one of those things—writer, dad, husband—he could manage with style. Maybe even two of them. But trying to be all three was beyond him.

So, here's how I'm going to finish the story this time:

Whitey cooks a delicious meal. French bread and cheese, roast chicken, salad. He opens the bottle of wine he took from my apartment and fills our glasses.

After taking a sip, I notice a Charlie Mingus record leaning against the bookshelf. Hey, I say excitedly, Mingus looks just like that Knuckleball Charlie guy I saw pitching in the desert I was just telling you about.

That's crazy, Whitey responds, without taking a moment to consider what I had said. Why would one of the most famous jazz men in the world waste his time doing something as meaningless as that?

Your dad loved Mingus. The chaotic mix of sounds and rhythms. Bullfighting music. He called it. Rattlesnake music. But I never liked a note Mingus played. I preferred the sinuous vine-like music of Paul Desmond. He was my honey man and always will be.

Chapter Four

THREE POUND HAMMER

[son]

A week after my mother dies, we have a yard sale in the driveway of her house. Paula and I set up tables and clothes racks and fill them with the leftovers of my mother's life.

I get uncomfortable when I see her wine-red embroidered blouse. Her long black evening dress. Her white dishes and cups. Her coffee maker and blender. Her print of California foothills in the gold frame. Her Sunset gardening books. Her silver cocktail shaker. It doesn't feel right. Each of these things, and all the other items we've put out for sale, are part of my private archive, they help me remember how my mother changed over the years. They shouldn't be set out on display for any neighbor or stranger to bargain for, or sneer at, or not even notice, as they search for something else that isn't there, some personal treasure or valuable prize.

Instead of a garage sale, I proposed that we pay someone to pack everything up and take it to Goodwill. Pay someone? Paula responded dismissively. Your mother wouldn't want us to do that. I'm sure of it.

I wasn't so sure. Yes, my mother had a practical side, but she had also been an intensely private person, and a proud person too. In the end, I agreed to the garage sale, but I never liked the idea.

Paula's stylish clothes and her red lipstick and her German accent keep the lowballing to a minimum. She smiles. She compliments. She chit-chats. She makes it clear that she is a professional and nobody can get anything over on her. We make a little money off the early wave of shoppers. When it slows down, we sit in the driveway, on a couple of folding chairs, drinking green tea from a thermos and snacking on Save Mart bagels and cream cheese.

Over there was the Meachum's house, I tell Paula, pointing across the street. Waiting for her eyes to move in that direction. They were Born Agains. And Charlie, the alcoholic bricklayer, lived next to them. He taught me how to make adobe bricks. More importantly, he had a cabin at Bass Lake where I lost my virginity. And my best friend, Steve, lived in that house on the corner, with the chain-link fence, before he changed his name to Janus. And Dale and her Mormon husband and their three tall sons lived in that house next to us, before they moved into the hills and opened a lodge. Rosa lives in their house now.

I can't figure out why I am telling Paula these things. Why I'm trying to make Brooks sound like an interesting street to grow up on, when it hadn't been. Besides, everyone who lived there when I was a kid has moved away or died. My mother was the last one left. The gringa with the green lawn and the loud jazz you could hear from the sidewalk.

Her house sits in an odd, almost sunken, triangular-shaped neighborhood, squeezed between a long irrigation ditch, the train tracks, and a busy road. Most of the houses are small, squat boxes. Many with fenced-in front yards of dirt or brown grass in which loud mean dogs keep unwanted visitors away.

While Paula sweet-talks a frumpy middle-aged woman interested in Mom's old microwave, I go inside to use the bathroom. Pausing at the top of the steps, I look past the houses at the end of the street and watch a freight train thundering along the tracks that cut a razor-sharp diagonal from West Ave to Fruit.

I make a mental note to tell Paula the story about when Steve and I were kids riding our bikes along the dirt path paralleling the tracks and a freight train screeched to a stop, its air horn wailing. Dust swirled in the air while we sat on our bikes, covering our eyes and coughing. A few minutes later the train started moving again. Steve jumped off his bike and yelled, run! He reached up and grabbed the metal ladder of a boxcar. I ran behind him and pulled myself up on the next ladder. I arched my back and turned my face into the wind and felt like I had conquered something. Then, I looked down at the blurry ground. Felt sick. And jumped. Tumbling head over heels in the gravely dirt. That ride couldn't have lasted more than a few minutes. And I never hopped a freight train again. Yet, that memory is still vivid almost fifty years later.

I open the front door and step inside. It's gut wrenching to see my mother's house stripped of everything she did to make it hers. To make it the truest representation of who she really was. Had been. Even who she wanted to be. Her magic and stagecraft have been sucked out of the rooms with such force that the house I grew up in feels strange and unfamiliar to me. The linoleum in the entryway is scuffed and covered with a thin layer of grit. The off-white walls are greasy and marred by handprints and cobwebs. The beige wall-to-wall carpet is stained and frayed.

I close my eyes and try to visualize the house as it had been the last time I was there with my mother. She sat on the sea-green couch, a frail woman with a pinched look on her face, struggling to put her thoughts into words.

For the first time in my life, I understand the impulse to seal up a room, or an entire house, after a loved one has passed away. To leave everything exactly as it was. I want nothing more than to drive away knowing that when I come back in a week or a month or a year, my mother's furry black slippers will be sitting in front of the wall heater; her maroon sweater will be hanging on the back of the yellow chair; and the kitchen table will be littered with piles of catalogs, magazines, newsletters, advertisements, and bills.

I step back outside and survey the yard sale crowd, wondering if I'll see someone I used to know. Paula holds center stage. Wheeling and dealing. I study the wrinkles radiating from her eyes and mouth, running across her forehead, crooked and lovely. She's talking to a young man about the cocktail shaker. My eyes drift down to her large breasts pushing against her red bra.

For a moment Lust, the great eraser, washes over me. *Forget about the money, let's go inside and make love!* I want to whisper to her.

She notices me staring at her. She winks, then turns around to take the young man's money. I'm not sure, but I think she wiggles her ass in my direction.

Her ass-wiggle and her beautiful breasts and her sly wink don't mean a thing.

Nor do the few hundred dollars we make.

The empty house and the ugly street tear into me.

I can't wait to get out of there.

A week later, I drive back to my mother's house to get rid of the items that hadn't sold and that were too large or heavy for Paula and me to take to Goodwill. I park in front of the house, then I unlock the door and stand at the front window.

A few minutes later, I hear Jan's Jeep rumble and cough around the corner. Then I hear the clanging of the U-Haul trailer bumping over the curb, as he backs into the driveway. Jan jumps out of his Jeep with a bag of donuts in one hand and a cardboard tray holding two coffees in the other. He's wearing a dark blue beret pulled down tight over his head and a faded blue sweatshirt with a torn sleeve zipped up to his neck.

He'd come to the garage sale, took some of mom's clothes, her blender, and a few pots and pans, not to mention Frankie and Whiskers, my mother's two cats. When he offered to come back and help me finish things up the next weekend, I couldn't say no. It was that or hire someone.

Damn, this is hard. He says, a few seconds later, when we are standing in the kitchen sipping coffee and eating donuts. How old was she anyway?

She died two days before her 84th birthday I tell him—and then I realize that I've been repeating that phrase, *two days before her 84th birthday*, to anyone who asked. To make it clear that she had lived a long life. And that I had provided in every possible way for her care. And that I had not subtracted a single day from her life through neglect or selfishness.

Jan looks down. His large brown eyes soften and for a moment I recognize the kid who played "Classical Gas" on his guitar with such delicate passion that I was sure he was going to be famous.

After coffee, we get started. First, we move the mattress and box springs from my old bedroom into the trailer. Then we lift the bulky couch and slowly carry it out of the living room. We work steadily, catching up as we go.

He's been divorced for years. He couldn't take living with the daughter of a Missionary Baptist minister. He asks about Paula and my life in Berkeley. He tells me that his son and his family just moved back to Fresno to find work. It's tough, he admits, but they're getting to know each other again.

I feel bad. Paula and I have had it so easy with Lily in comparison. I tell him that we go to Germany almost every year and that Lily speaks fluent German. He nods, says that's great, then he lifts a heavy chair in a bear hug, and carries it out to the trailer by himself.

In no time at all we've emptied the living room and the middle bedroom and my mother's bedroom. That leaves the Wedgwood. The Wedgwood is cast iron and white porcelain with two ovens and a griddle between the burners. My mother bought it used in the 1960s. I never understood how she got it home and inside her tiny kitchen.

From my perspective it had always been there. The rest of the kitchen changed over the years. The sink, the refrigerator, the dishwasher, the linoleum, the color of the walls and the cabinets. But not the Wedgwood.

Jan turns off the gas and disconnects the line. We pull the stove a few feet away from the wall. Now what? I ask, feeling a jolt of pain shoot up my back. Don't worry, Jan says, I've got a furniture dolly in the jeep.

I watch him center the dolly and cinch a strap around the large white stove. He muscles it up until it's balanced, then we inch it forward until it pushes against the door frame and stops.

Shit! It doesn't fit! Maybe we should just leave it.

Jan laughs in disbelief, then motions me out of the way. No way, man. We're getting this sucker out of here one way or another.

He taps the thin edge of a crowbar with a hammer, working it under the door trim. Then he gently rocks the crowbar back and forth popping the trim off in one long strip that he rests against the wall.

That's when it hits me that this is probably the last time I will ever stand inside my mother's house. While Jan works on the doorway, I walk down the dingy hallway to her bedroom. I notice the dusty outlines the pictures have left on the walls. I stare at the marks of the headboard in the paint, and at the queen-size rectangle of darker carpet where the bed had been.

The last few weeks she was home my mother couldn't get out of bed without my help. I'd squat in front of her and wait for her to put her arms on my shoulders. Then I'd slowly stand up, lifting her off the bed, and walk with her to the bathroom. When she was finished, I helped her get dressed. Slipping her panties far enough up her thighs that she could reach them, followed by a pair of old sweats, a top and a light sweater. I felt a surprising sense of gratitude sharing these intimacies with her. Being able to. When I had been so sure I would fail.

I stand at the door of her bathroom. I stare inside her walk-in closet. I pause at the sliding glass door leading to the garden. Desperate to feel the slightest hint of her presence. But the only thing speaking to me is the house itself, going through its own process of withdrawal and transformation. Of course, her house is traumatized. Fifty years is a long time to be lived in by one person.

Once Jan is finished, we tilt the Wedgwood back on the dolly and slowly roll it over the threshold, setting it down outside, at the top of the stairs. Jan hurries over to his Jeep, pulls it forward, then cranks the wheel and backs up at a sharp angle. We work the stove forward until it slides over the edge of the stairs and slams into the back of the trailer. Jan straps everything down, then we go inside and drink some water from the kitchen faucet.

Your mom was quite a woman. I'm really going to miss her. Jan finally says, breaking the silence. She had a great sense of humor and a curious mind. And she always listened to me, no matter how far out there I got.

I look at Jan and marvel. It's been nearly forty years since I moved out of my mother's house. Forty-five years since he lived on the corner. How is it possible, after all this time, that the last person to stand with me in my mother's house, is this near total stranger, who at one time had been my best friend? I am thankful beyond words that he is here with me.

Back in Berkeley, I plan a small memorial for my mother. I have a list of people to invite, like her friend Marie in Phoenix and Linda in Santa Cruz and Mary in Fresno and Pat, her brother Edward's last wife, in Virginia, and, of course, Jan. But I don't invite any of them. Or anyone else.

I want to, and Paula says she'll help. But in the end, I don't do anything. Except scan a stack of photographs of and tape them to the wall. For days I wander in and out of the dining room looking at the photos. I don't have the faintest idea how they relate to each other. How they add up, or what they have to say about the world my mother lived in for 84 years.

The person in the photographs looks so different photo to photo that it feels like they are pictures of different people. In the end, the gallery is more painful than a memorial would have been. There is no catharsis, no commiseration, just a cold and ever deepening suspicion that my mother had been a stranger to me, as I must have been to her.

A few weeks later, Paula removes the photos without asking. Time to move on, George, she states with authority. Then she leads me down the stairs to the garage and says, I think it's time we bring some of your mom's stuff into the house.

I'm shocked. I didn't think Paula liked my mother's things. First, we carry the dark oak credenza that stood in my mother's hallway, and place it in our hallway. Then we move the tall pine cabinet with glass doors that spent many years in my mother's kitchen, behind the Formica table, into our dining room. After that, we bring up the heavy yellow and red wooden chairs and place them at both ends of our long dining room table.

Once we finish with the furniture, we unpack the few pieces of art my mother accumulated over the years. Pieces I had stood in front of many times and scrutinized as I grew up, and even after I moved away. Pieces that marked the brief period in her life, before my father died, when art and people making art mattered, and the long stretch of the rest of her life when having these pieces reminded her, and me, that such a life was possible.

There's a charcoal drawing of a woman washing her hair in a large metal bucket, which we hang in our upstairs bathroom. And a pencil sketch of two cats sitting on stairs, elongated and smiling—drawn in a cartoonish, almost cubist style—which we hang in the entry way, so that it is visible when you first enter our house. Then there is the most precious piece of all, one that predates the others. A small pastel drawing by my mother's Scottish grandfather—whose name was also George—of tiny brown sailing ships flying red and white flags crossing choppy green waves. We place the pastel on the mantel above the fireplace.

Not only can I see it every time I walk in or out of the living room, but I can also pick it up and examine the inscription on the back whenever I like.

In this way Paula and I move as much of my mother's house into our house as possible. Making a home within a home. And giving me the sense that my mother's house lives on in ours.

Over the ensuing weeks a day rarely passes that I don't take a moment to appreciate the presence of my mother's things. They make me feel less guilty about not organizing a memorial. In a sense, I feel like I have done much more than that by bringing her belongings into my daily life.

But this equilibrium doesn't last. Our day, Lily leaves my great-grandfather's pastel lying on the floor. Shortly after that, Paula moves a large plant in front of the sketch of the elongated cats. Then I find the red chair in the garage and the yellow chair upstairs. I want to say something to Paula and Lily, but I feel like I shouldn't have to.

After that, my office becomes my refuge. There is a healing quality to the light that streams through the two large windows. But more than that, there is the fact that nobody ever puts anything in or takes anything out of my office. If I leave a coffee cup on my desk, there it sits. If I spread a stack of photographs out on the table behind my desk nobody touches them or covers them up or rearranges them.

To preserve the sense that I'm simultaneously living in my house and my mother's, I move my great-grandfather's pastel into my office and set it on the bookshelf. I hang the cat sketch on the picture wire behind my desk. I set the drawing of the woman in the wash bucket on my desk to the right of my computer screen.

I begin to spend more and more time in my office. Sitting in my chair, looking at these things, not thinking about the past or the future. One morning, after I pull the shades up and turn on the portable heater because it's a cold, damp day—outside the rain is soft and fuzzy like liquid moss and fresh white buds cover the neighbor's magnolia—I swivel around in my chair and study the row of photographs hanging next to the cat drawing.

One catches my eye. Paula and my mother facing each other, both in profile, at Aquatic Park in San Francisco. Paula wearing a thick-ribbed white sweater with a high collar, biting her lip. My mother bundled up in an oversized green sweatshirt, arms folded, lost in thought. The late afternoon sun casts a soft warm glow on both of their faces. I notice Paula's expression. It's touchingly clear how much she loves my mother.

Then I lower my glance and see my mother's old computer still sitting under my desk, next to a stack of Bankers Boxes. I had planned to get rid of it right away, then I decided I should at least boot it up once, to check if there is anything on it that I wanted to save. Besides, I had come to wonder if her computer might be the last place my mother existed in any tangible sense. Her voice might still be there. Evidence of her quirky mind. Images from her life. I couldn't get rid of all that.

Come on, George. I chide myself, stop being so wishy-washy. Just remove the hard drive and save it for later. Then bury the rest of the computer in the backyard, next to the dead dogs and cats. I even imagine Paula, Lily and I standing in a circle, performing a ceremony or ritual for her old machine. But something about burying my mother's computer in our backyard feels creepy. Then a different thought pops into my head and I call a crematorium. The young woman who answers informs me in a slightly irritated but professional voice that computers are full of toxic materials. We can't take it, she adds, then hangs up.

Fine! I shout into the empty room.

That's when I notice the postcard that says, *Now's the Time!* in black type on a white background, leaning against a stack of unread books. I had taken that postcard from the bulletin board in my mother's computer room. Maybe it's time to listen to the postcard, I decide.

I move a stack of books from my desk to the floor. I gather the writing I am working on into one pile and old paperwork into another. I lift her computer and put it on my desk. I set up the screen and connect her keyboard and mouse. Then I push the power button, lean back in my chair, and wait. Outside the rain is pounding. When I look at the screen a few seconds later, an empty rectangle with a faint vertical line is blinking on and off, prompting me to enter a password. I stare blankly at the screen for a few seconds.

Then I remember flipping through a green notebook before putting it in the Bankers Box labeled MOM – Correspondence, Notebooks, Phone Books. I remember seeing a page of usernames and passwords. I find the notebook, locate the page of passwords, and underline the entry referring to her computer. Much to my surprise, the password works.

For a moment, I remember all the times I helped my mother fix something on her computer. Deleting old files that were filling up her hard drive. Updating virus definitions. Showing her how to add a photo to an email. Her computer was her lifeline. An important part of her daily routine. Especially after her friends stopped writing letters.

I click on Internet Explorer, which automatically loads her AOL email program. The subject lines of dozens of messages scroll down the screen. The font extra-large so she could read it. A lot of messages arrived after she died, which shouldn't surprise me, but does. I think big tech should be smart enough for that not to happen.

Then, I notice a message from Jan dated, Monday, November 30th. The very day he had helped me clean out my mother's house. A little further down is another message from Jan, dated Saturday, November 28th. And another from Friday the 27th. And one from Thursday, November 26th, Thanksgiving. Five days after she died. Why was Jan emailing my mother? He knew she was dead.

I open the Thanksgiving email. He tells her not to worry, he's canceled their dinner reservation at Fish

Camp Lodge. It breaks my heart, he writes. I can't believe you're gone. My life is split open. I'm sorry, I can't let you go. I'm going to keep emailing you until they shut your systems down.

My hands drop from the keyboard and fall limply on my lap. I stare out the window. Stunned, as if a flash bulb has just gone off in my face. The words THEY WERE LOVERS light up in my head like a neon sign. My mother and my childhood friend were lovers! I feel shame and panic. I want to delete all the messages. And not say anything to anyone about their relationship. Not even Paula.

Why shame? I hear a voice ask inside my cavernous head. What is there for you to be ashamed of? So what if your mother was sleeping with the same person she made peanut butter and jelly sandwiches for when you were kids. Then I realize where the shame is coming from.

A few days after cleaning out Mom's house, Jan called to check on me. He was worried and wanted to know if I was doing alright. The world is a crazy place, old friend, he told me toward the end of the conversation. Crazy shit is happening all around us that you probably aren't aware of, living in a place like Berkeley. You might not know that the government is adding mind control chemicals to the clouds. Or that the super-rich are manipulating the markets and if you don't want to lose everything you've worked for, you need to buy gold. Or that swarms of invaders are pushing against the border and will be here soon.

You don't know any of this because you're living in a bubble where the future looks rosy and you can afford to tune all the scary shit out.

The reality of how different we were opened up like a chasm and I was speechless. So, the truth is, I am ashamed of Jan. Ashamed that he is the kind of man my mother wanted by her side at the end of her life. And then, almost instantaneously, I am ashamed that I am ashamed.

A few nights later Paula and I watch a film about an old man who leaves Mexico City for a small mountainous village where he has decided to commit suicide.

Once he is in the village he rents a room from a woman, even older than he is, who owns a small farm on a hill. He sleeps on a bed in her barn. She cooks for him and washes his clothes. After a couple of days, he asks her a favor. Will she have sex with him?

The next day she agrees. She undresses and sits on the edge of the bed. I turn away from the sight of her naked body. What's the matter? Paula teases me. She doesn't look that bad.

It's true. The old woman is soft and small and ancient. Her face is round and sad. She removes her jewelry and places it on the table next to the bed. She fluffs up her hair. The old man kneels at the foot of the bed and tries to get her to turn over on her stomach. To lift her hips in the air. But she can't do it. So he leans her back on the mattress and climbs on top of her, pressing his knees between her legs. He moves slowly, deliberately, like a photographer positioning a subject for a portrait.

Watching the old woman's breasts flopping over her arms, her face turned, staring blankly at me, her dirty face scarred with rough lines and nicks and crevices, her thin knees raised slightly, ready for the old man to enter her, I can't help but feel like I'm watching Jan in bed with my mother.

Jan is methodical and careful. His actions look more like physical therapy than sex. That's how I want to imagine it, anyway. But maybe my mother wrapped her arms around Jan and pulled him inside her. And held him there. Maybe the film is trying to remind me that passion is what really matters. Not beauty or love. That passion is the body's fullest expression.

A couple days later I watch the movie a second time and I am astonished to see that it is distributed by Janus Films. The first time I watched it, I hadn't noticed the emblem of an ancient Roman coin showing the two-headed god projected against the black background.

I had also forgotten that once the old man is having sex with her, the woman starts to move in rhythm with him, even lifting her head and shoulders off the bed, toward the man, who braces himself to keep his upper body from touching hers. And that she grabs one of his hands and presses it against her breast. And that the man lacks all passion until he finishes and begins sobbing. And that the woman cradles his head and runs her fingers through his thick gray hair.

Another week passes, and I still don't know what to do about my mother's emails. I'm not ready to delete them. And printing them out feels wrong. I don't want that much tangibility in my house, even in an unmarked file, or a sealed manila envelope. That feels like collecting evidence and what do I need evidence for?

My inability to decide gives Paula a chance to read Jan's emails. At first, she's happy to learn that my mother had someone to love when we she was old and alone. Paula feels vindicated, even. Because one time she told me that she thought my mother had a secret lover and I had refused to believe her.

The more Paula reads, however, the more upset she becomes. What a manipulator, she says harshly. Such an asshole. One day he's just got to come over to see her, and the next three days he doesn't even respond to her messages. And then when he does, he tries to force his crazy conspiracy theories on your mom. George, this guy is a creep! You've got to do something.

Paula's reaction triggers a memory. I'm sitting at a small table in someone's kitchen in my early twenties. A woman stands at the sink washing dishes wearing a fuzzy white bath robe. She has short red hair and a pale blotchy face. I think her name is Sherry and that she's from Texas and that she's studying to be an opera singer in Fresno.

Steve went out with Sherry for a few months. After they broke up, he introduced us. A little while later we started dating. Since I had known Steve for so long Sherry felt comfortable complaining about him to me. She'd say, he's so insecure. And jealous. And a liar. She went on and on like this for weeks. Then she stopped. I thought she had exhausted the subject of Steve and was ready to move on with me.

What had actually happened, I learned later, was that Steve started calling Sherry, and showing up at her door late at night insisting she let him in, and threatening to make a scene and wake the neighbors if she didn't. They'd sit on her couch or in her kitchen and he'd tell her how much he missed her, and what a mistake he had made letting her go, and he'd question her about what it was like sleeping with his best friend. Then he'd start rubbing her shoulders and back and try to undress her.

Sherry admitted all this to me months later, scrunched up in the far corner of her couch. Confessing between sobs that Steve had been coming over two or three times a week, late and night, and forcing her to have sex with him. I'm miserable, she screamed. I can't take it anymore. You both need to leave me alone!

When I tell Paula this, she is furious. You need to confront Steve or Janus or whatever his name is!

That was a long time ago, I remind her. He was a disturbed young man, that doesn't mean he's still like that.

Some things don't change, George. You need to tell him that you remember how he treated Sherry.

Just to make him nervous about what else you might know.

Okay, I say. Maybe.

A few days later Paula busts into my office highly agitated and demands that I get rid of my mother's hard drive. NOW!

I can't have all that hate speech sitting around so close to my bed anymore!

But I haven't saved her emails yet.

Just bury it, she shouts, unable to hold back any longer.

Okay! Whatever! I blurt out.

I'm actually relieved. Happy to let her make the decision. I pull the cover off the computer and quickly unscrew the mount that holds the hard drive in place.

Paula grabs the drive out of my hand and wraps it in one of my mother's colorful scarves. Follow me, she commands, and marches downstairs and into the backyard. I stop at the garage and pick up a shovel and a three-pound sledgehammer. Paula unwraps the hard drive and sits it on the bricks underneath the fig tree. I kneel, raise the hammer, and slam it down on the drive, over and over again. The adrenalin and catharsis shoot through my neck and shoulders like an otherworldly massage.

When a corner of a brick chips off and nearly hits Paula in the eye, I pick up the severely dented drive and shake it to make sure I can hear the internal parts rattling around inside the palm-sized shell before handing it to Paula.

She tells me to dig a hole next to my mother's fake headstone. When I'm finished, Paula drops the hard drive in. I fill the hole up with dirt and tamp it down. I scatter some small stones mixed with dead leaves over it. Paula pushes a stick into the ground and wraps my mother's scarf around it.

The fog blowing through the Golden Gate begins to clear and patches of blue sky appear overhead as we walk up the stairs to the deck. I pause for a step or two and gaze up at the sky.

Burying my mother's hard drive after pummeling it to smithereens with a sledgehammer was far more satisfying than a memorial party could ever have been.

In the living room, I want to jump on Paula's back and swing her around and around in accelerating circles until we both take flight into the sky like two birds become one.

I should probably say that I have forgiven my mother and Jan. But the truth is I no longer think about their affair in terms of guilt or forgiveness. I see it as a kind of offering. Something to turn over and over in my head and study from different perspectives for as long as I live. Their affair feels like a seed which if planted in the right soil, and given a proper amount of water and sunlight, will grow into a different kind of story, purged of all the shame and anger it originally produced.

I think about visiting Jan in Porterville. Not letting on that I know he had been sleeping with my mother. I see myself studying his hands and the reverberation of his voice. The voice of the two-faced god, the god of childhood and manhood. We exchange memories of my mother. He plays a tune on his guitar that he's writing as a tribute to her. We walk to a 7-Eleven and buy snacks, like we did when we were kids.

Then I imagine myself hugging Jan goodbye and driving home. Once I'm outside of Porterville, I pull-over and sit in my car, surrounded by orange trees. I grab my laptop from my backpack and start typing—the hoped-for story flows through my fingers.

When I try to explain all of this to Paula it sounds so abstract and confusing that I get flustered and change the subject. I can tell she doesn't like it. She's upset because she thinks I'm going to let Jan off the hook—which, in the end, I suppose, is exactly what I do.

Chapter Five

MY CALIFORNIA

[mom]

I used to think that being on the same wavelength was a metaphor. But it's quite literal. Like different spectrums of light, some visible to humans, some not.

George and I were always close, but not necessarily on the same wavelength. Now it's like we're playing Marco Polo and he's wearing the blindfold. I keep moving, inches away from his fingers, almost willing him to touch me, and he keeps abruptly changing directions, darting this way and that.

One of the things I remember most about George is how he always liked to surprise me. Usually, I played along, but I often wondered, why are you going to all this trouble?

The incident I'm thinking about now occurred one afternoon in Berkeley. George got all excited and said, you'll never guess where I'm going to take you. But I didn't feel like guessing because there didn't seem to be any reason for him not to just tell me.

I let George help me down the brick stairs from his front porch to the sidewalk. Taking one slow step at a time, I noticed the dull green moss growing between the cracks and worried that George would slip and fall and take me down with him. When we reached his BMW station wagon, he opened the passenger-side door and waited for me to get in, which wasn't easy because of how low to the ground that car was.

Without saying a word, George started the engine and drove slowly into the hills, hunched forward and concentrating, like he was trying to find his way out of a maze. A few blocks up one steep street, a tentative right turn, another right turn, a few more blocks up another steep street, a number of left turns, a couple more right turns, climbing steadily.

Finally, we reached the summit, and I took a moment to admire the water far below. I recognized the Bay Bridge and Alcatraz and San Francisco. But there were other islands I didn't know the name of, and a long finger of a pier I couldn't place, and another bridge far off to the right. It was breathtaking, even though the air was a dirty orange color.

A few minutes later, George made an abrupt right turn, and we started a long swooping descent. It felt like I was in a glider buffeted by heavy turbulence. It was so disorienting I had to shut my eyes and clutch the hard plastic armrest. When I opened them again, I was dizzy and confused. George didn't notice. He kept finding ever smaller, ever windier streets to turn onto.

After so many years in Fresno, I had gotten used to the grid. The grid was comforting. One set of parallel streets running north and south intersected by another set of parallel streets running east and west. I always knew where I was in relation to where I had come from and where I wanted to go. But the Berkeley city planners poo-pooed the grid. So did George.

When the road finally straightened out, I was relieved to see that we were in a neighborhood of fine old houses with large, manicured yards. George turned left one last time and parked. I had no idea what he was up to.

He hopped out of the car and opened my door. He took my arm and we slowly walked across the wide sidewalk to an elegant iron fence. I peered up at a large green house sitting on a sloping hill with big windows and dark gables and towering brick chimneys.

Then it hit me: this was the Lanza house. What a shock to my system to be standing there again after so many years. The house hadn't changed. But it wasn't the same either.

George stood next to me, fidgeting, rubbing his hands together, like he expected a total metamorphosis of thanks. Like he thought my old body would spontaneously combust in gratitude, and my 7-year-old self would be standing in its place, ready to burst into song.

What the hell, George?

Then it dawned on me that he must have thought that those few weeks I spent at the Lanza's with my mother in 1939 had planted the seed of California in my head and set the course for my entire life, which was simply ridiculous. One thing leads to another is how it really happens. And the earlier experiences are no more important than the later ones.

Well, Mom?

Well, George?

Do you recognize the house?

Of course, I recognize it. I'm old, not senile.

I was almost 75. I didn't feel like playing games with my son. Besides, I was getting a little uncomfortable. If George had found the Lanza house that meant he'd been doing research, and that meant he probably had a dossier containing everything he could dig up about Horace Lanza and my aunts Selena and Maude and their old house in Piedmont, as well as many other wonderful and fascinating facts about my family, which sooner or later he would torment me with. That was fine. George was just being George. But he had a certain cluelessness about my life. My decisions. My corners backed into. And settled into.

I turned away and took a long look down the tree-lined street and my frustration faded—there was my 7-year-old-self, clear as day, playing with a neighbor girl in a large grassy yard down the street. We watched a stream of elegantly dressed women walk in and out of an oversized gingerbread house on the corner. Pretending it was our house and they were our servants.

I must admit, I was tickled George had brought me back to the Lanza house, which, at one time, had been part of my family.

George looked at his phone. It was time to pick Lily up from volleyball practice at the high school around the corner.

I'll wait here; I impulsively told him.

As soon as George drove off, I knew I had made a mistake. I felt unsettled, not sure why I wanted to be alone with the Lanza house. Sure, I spent a lot of time alone in Fresno. But that was different. My house wasn't just comfortable and safe. It helped me manage a lifetime of memories, to keep them flowing harmoniously, so that remembering felt like watching a popular ballet. Never too boring or too frightening.

I gripped the iron bars of the fence for balance and tried to settle myself down by thinking about that summer, which had begun when I got on the train with my mother in Detroit.

The floors of the train were freshly mopped, and the metal walls were gleaming. I remember I was so excited to be going to California that I kept pestering my mother with questions as we walked down the aisle to our compartment. She wore a cranberry-red dress that fit her perfectly and made her short slender body look sophisticated and summery. She had made me wear an old blue dress which drooped from my shoulders straight down to my calves.

Whenever I think about that train ride two things always pop into my head. White gloves and poker. Women wore white gloves to the dining car. Men sat up late in their pressed shirts, their wide ties and their stiff hats, smoking and playing cards.

I was a fidgety girl. When my mother couldn't take my squirming and my rattling on and on any longer, she'd send me to the lounge car to find someone my own age to talk to. Sometimes I did find a young girl or boy who was just as bored as I was. When there were no kids, I'd walk up and down the aisle babbling about what I saw outside the train window or telling everyone that I was going to the big fair in California.

I was a regular Chatty Cathy.

A motor mouth from Motor City.

The women sitting around drinking and gossiping in their white gloves and fine hats usually ignored me. Some of the men laughed when I passed by. Others tried to get rid of me or at least make me shut up. Finally, one of the men hit on the idea of teaching me how to play poker, promising me a milkshake if I could keep quiet for the entire game. Once the game started, he leaned over and told me in a low, very serious voice, that I would have to be very, very quiet, if I wanted that milkshake. Much to that man's surprise, I came close to winning that first hand. I've loved poker ever sense.

As we sped across the country, my mother entertained herself by snapping orders at me. I need another tissue, dear. Go get me a coffee. Black with two sugars. And don't forget today's paper, or I'll send you back out again.

She also tried out different voices on me. There was the silky sophisticated salesclerk voice. The soft pleading, darling could you. . . voice. The exasperated mother voice calibrated to make me feel like my very presence was draining the life out of her.

It wasn't until my dad died and she moved to Atlanta with Charlie the shoe salesman and started speaking like a southern belle that she finally got comfortable with her voice. That was her second life. Second husband. Second family. Second landscape and culture. I hardly knew her then.

Staring at the front gardens of the Lanza house, I remembered George telling me how much he enjoyed traveling by train. He said it freed his mind and got his creative juices flowing. He'd ridden trains through Europe and Canada and Mexico and Asia, but not much in the States.

George thought that train ride must have made a great impression on me, because it was the first time

I had ever left Michigan. He liked to regale me with questions about all the things I might have seen. My first prairie. My first oceanic wheat field. My first purple mountain range. But I didn't experience the train ride that way. I was either bored blind and it felt like we were slowly moving through a gray tunnel. Or I was daydreaming, and details popped up before my eyes like spring-loaded billboards.

There's my new bicycle!

My house with a mile-long driveway!

My adorable collie!

My new best friend!

My speedy horse!

My lake!

My super tall pine tree!

My moon!

In between these Technicolor flashes I didn't see anything. It wasn't even a blur, just blank space in my head.

When the train arrived in Oakland, I wasn't sure what to expect. It was dark outside. Fog billowed over the buildings and the windows of the train were covered with drops of water. My mother stood stiff and motionless in the hallway waiting for the train to come to a stop. I stood next to her. She had spent hours in front of the mirror that afternoon, meticulously applying her makeup and fussing with her short brown hair until it was perfect, then putting on one of the fancy hats from the department store where she worked and pinning it down at just the right angle to accentuate her delicate face and pretty brown eyes.

She was nervous. We weren't visiting her family, after all. No one in her family had ever left Michigan, except her French-Canadian father who vanished back over the border shortly after she was born. We were visiting daddy's two sisters, Selena and Maude. And daddy wasn't with us.

I was staring up the long driveway at what the Lanzas had called the carriage house when George returned with Lily. George told her that I had lived in this house when I was a little girl.

Visited, I corrected him.

Still sweaty from her volleyball practice, Lily dropped her backpack on the sidewalk and looked up at the big house. I wanted to tell her something about that wonderful summer, but I didn't know where to begin. One thing was clear, she didn't want to stand there any longer than necessary. Finally, I pointed at the end of the driveway and said, see that giant redwood tree behind the garage? That was the very first redwood I ever saw in my life.

Lily looked at the tree for a few seconds, then she looked back at me and said, it must have been a really tiny tree way back then.

There had been a time when Lily and I would have stood in front of that gate making up stories about the Lanzas and their big house—and George would have been the one to get impatient. But Lily's mind was rewiring itself and she no longer had time for sharing stories with her grandmother.

On the way home, George started telling me everything he had learned about Mr. Lanza, which was pretty much what I had expected him to do. Did you know Mr. Lanza came from a rich family in New York. And that he moved to California to become a wine maker, against his parent's wishes. And that Mr. Lanza owned a vineyard in Napa Valley and another large house up there. Mr. Lanza must have been 10 times, even 100 times, richer than anyone you had ever met. What was it like for a poor girl from Detroit to stay in a house like that?

George was right, I had never even glanced inside a house as grand as the Lanza's. George kept talking and talking until his voice started to sound like a TV commercial and I tuned him out. By then, the big houses rolling by had morphed into strange little advertisements of their own.

Every yard was a picture-perfect paradise calling my name. *Georgiana, you look so tired, why don't you lie down here*, one garden murmured. *Sink into my green light. Drown in my creek near the picturesque foot bridge* another one called out. *No, no, Georgiana, it's much better to die here.* The voice of the next garden whispered. *Buried in a profusion of bright jungle flowers. Don't do it,* moaned a 400-year-old oak in the next yard. *The jungle will quickly devour you. Your memories will survive much longer in the gentle light filtering through my thick branches. Don't listen to that old tree, Georgiana.* The next yard protested. *What better resting place could there be than my half-acre of manicured Kentucky bluegrass, enclosed in a four-foot stone wall. Think of all the sunny days to come if you leave your burdens here.*

Enough, I silently shouted.

George was still droning on and on when I started paying attention again. He said that the Lanza house had sold for five million dollars to a Chinese investor just a few years ago. What got my attention was the phrase, *just a few years ago.*

Maybe Selena and Horace's children, or their grandchildren, or great-grandchildren, had lived there all that time. They were all that was left of daddy's family. Why hadn't I tried harder to stay in touch?

At a stoplight, George turned the radio down and repeated a question he had apparently already asked.

How about eating at a nice Italian restaurant tonight?

Oh, that sounds lovely. That's what I said, but I wasn't hungry, and I knew there was little chance that my appetite would improve any time soon.

George drove past a strip mall with a Safeway and a Pet Food Express, past a construction site for an apartment building. George drove right next to large, gleaming hospital complex, with bright colors arranged like artwork on the outside of the buildings, then turned right.

Aunt Selena and Aunt Maude. Two small, stout women, who dressed in fine but simple clothing.

Who had a chauffeur, a maid, a cook, and a gardener. Whose house was full of Persian carpets, oil paintings, colorful Italian glass bowls. Who had a garden with more flowers than I had ever seen in one place. Two old women with sing-song Scottish accents.

Selena had Mr. Lanza. But Maude was what they used to call a spinster. Nowadays she might have married a woman. Or maybe she just preferred being alone. The rhythm of their house was gentle and easy like sunshine warming the grass or slow-moving clouds fleecing the sky.

Lily grabbed her bag and dashed inside as soon as we parked. George took my arm and guided me up the brick stairs and then walked me over to the gray couch. I asked him if he could put on some music and get me some cheese and crackers and a beer.

The Lanza garden sparkling with warmth and sweetness, butterflies and hummingbirds, pine and sea salt and soothing breezes, had been my first taste of California. A big house with open doors and windows. Terraced hillside, a pool, lunches in the garden, a fountain, the glittering bay dotted with white sails. I was dazzled.

Not just by the house and the gardens but by how life was lived there. Gentle, big-hearted motion, was everywhere. The Italian cook bringing us fresh strawberries and warm sweet rolls for breakfast. The Japanese gardener pushing his yellow wheelbarrow full of dark soil. The maid throwing open the tall bedroom windows and shouting something in Spanish. Selena smiling and winking at me on the patio. Maude picking up a book and reading. Selena and Maude were the most relaxed adults I had ever met.

My own California came much later, not a big house near the Bay, but a small one in a dry valley turned into a farmer's paradise. Slowly, my Fresno yard became every bit as sweet as the Lanza's. Pink roses, oranges, a peach tree, and grapevines. Bonsai, cacti, Japanese maple, a weeping willow. Cats, a duck, rabbits, and a dog.

It had never crossed my mind that the Lanza House could change from being a place in my past to a place in George's present. It boggled the imagination. Now George drove by the Lanza house a couple times a week on the way to Lily's volleyball practice. He never stepped inside, but still that house was part of his life.

I found it amazing that after all this time George lived just a few miles from the Lanza house. What were the chances of that? I mean, it's a big country and an awful lot can happen in nearly seventy years.

George is nowhere near as rich as Mr. Lanza, but still his life isn't all that different, especially compared to mine in Fresno. Walk up to the top of his street and you can see San Francisco Bay, just like I could from the upstairs windows in the Lanza house. Walk around the block and there are towering redwoods and massive oak trees and bubbling creeks just like I remembered in Piedmont.

George came back into the living room and asked if I'd like to lie down before going to the restaurant.

I was a little miffed. Why couldn't he just let me be. But I had to admit, lying down sounded pretty good. I got settled on the daybed in Paula's office, under a fuzzy warm blanket, and absentmindedly gazed through the French doors at a jagged line of trees, while I half-listened to George and Paula and Lily move around in the house. Talking on the phone, opening the refrigerator, turning the faucet on upstairs, shooing a dog off the couch, all the little things that go on and on in a house full of people.

Just as I was about to fall asleep, Paula burst into the room, then apologized. She rummaged around on her desk, covered with piles of papers and pairs of glasses, bundles of fabric and other things that seemed to have been there a long time. I started to work my legs over the side of the bed.

Don't hurry, there's plenty of time before dinner, Paula reassured me. Then she left with her laptop and a pair of glasses.

I laid my head back down on the pillow and looked up at the tangerine ceiling and tangerine walls. The sun was shining through the French doors, and it felt like I was lying inside a sunbeam. I fell into a deep sleep and starting dreaming.

Mr. Lanza was taking us to the Golden Gate International Exposition on Treasure Island. We were in his huge black car driving across the Bay Bridge. Mr. Lanza sat in the passenger seat up front, and Mother and I were in back. Mother sat stiffly, head turned, staring out of the window, maybe at all the sailing ships and freighters on the Bay. Or at the wondrous new bridges. Or the stream of shiny cars, most from Detroit, and most with their windows rolled down and one or more elbows sticking out into the wind.

We got off the bridge and drove down to the island. I couldn't believe how beautiful San Francisco looked floating over the water just a short distance away. I stood next to the car and took a moment to soak in all the loveliness surrounding me. The bay was rough and wild and vast, the horizon curved, the brand new Golden Gate bridge in the distance looked like a tiny silhouette of paper, and the green hills behind it, and the long smudge of hills bending on the other side of the bay, formed a perfect circle around me.

I dreamt we were walking down a flag-lined promenade. Mother was wearing an emerald green dress. Mr. Lanza had on a light blue suit and a crisp white shirt. I finally got to wear the one good dress I had brought with me from Detroit. White with puffy sleeves. Maude loaned me her yellow scarf and Selena gave me her creamy sunhat and a pair of sunglasses.

I was so excited to finally go to the fair that I kept interrupting Mr. Lanza with questions. Is it true that there's a glittering tower of jewels so tall that people can see it in China? And that there's a rocket that will take you all the way to the moon and back? And that you can dance with lions and tigers in a crystal ball-room for only 25 cents?

Mr. Lanza looked down at me like a kind old priest, his thick grayish-white hair flowing over his head like a soft blurry photograph of water in motion.

Maybe in the future, he answered. Then he turned to my mother and started telling her how expensive the bridges had been to build, and how the Great Depression hadn't been nearly as bad in San Francisco as it had been in Detroit, and the possibility of a new war.

My mother let go of my hand and I slowly drifted behind them. I stopped at a large reflecting pool. Beyond it I saw a soaring tower with a ring of colossal men and women linked arm in arm near the top. Above them, stood a golden statue of a woman with wings—slender and strong—gleaming in the sun.

George, I could hear you calling me, trying to wake me for dinner. I turned toward your voice, trying to find the seam, the gap, the bright colorful light. But I had lost my way.

I was stuck in a sprawling garden drinking a large glass of iced tea inside a galaxy of redolent yellow flowers. A troop of hummingbirds arrived to repair my memory. The sun soaked into my bones and every part of me was expanding.

Chapter Six

GRIEF INFINITELY SUBDIVIDED

[son]

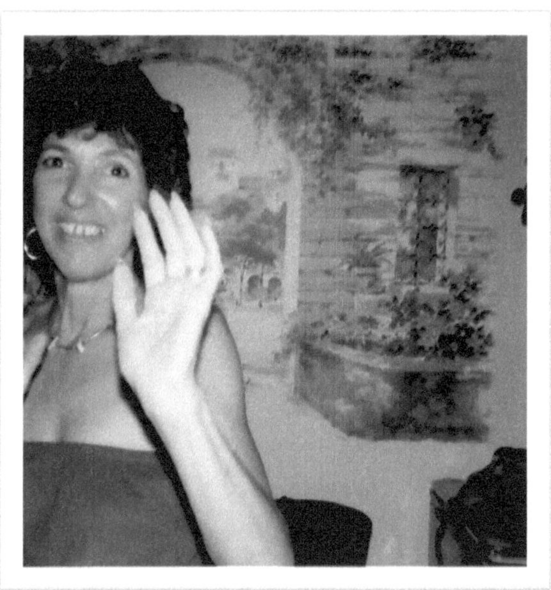

Part of my grieving process involved listening to a lot of Chinese music. Well not just Chinese music. Japanese and other Asian music too. Especially Asian Improv. A hybrid of jazz and Asian music, which reminded me of the first time I lived in San Francisco's Mission District. Before Paula and I got married and Lily was born.

Back then I thought I was honoring my parent's bohemian past. Exploring the ragged city, going out to live jazz and poetry readings, hunkering down in my rickety apartment, trying to write my own poetry.

But my life could hardly be compared to theirs. I wasn't married with a kid, with no steady income, chasing the now-you-see-it-now-you-don't American dollar wherever it took them. I had a real job with health insurance and all the rest of it.

I don't really understand why my obsession with Asian music went as far as it did, but I do know that it started with a stack of Bankers Boxes. Each labeled in my sloppy handwriting.

MOM – Notebooks, Letters, Etc.
MOM – Correspondence, Notebooks,
      Phone Books
MOM – Photos
MOM – CDs
MOM – Mail, Bills
MOM – MOM – MOM

The boxes sat there, stacked in our living room, for months. Visible to anyone coming into the house. Paula had been extremely patient. She knew I was afraid that if I put the boxes away, I would forget all about them, and by extension all about my mother, and that sooner or later both the boxes and my memories would rot and become useless.

Paula finally said something late one Sunday morning, while sitting in the orange chair under the small rectangular window next to the fireplace, reading the *New York Times,* and drinking green tea in a large white mug. I think it's time to do something with the boxes, George.

Alright, I responded unemotionally, and left the room.

Lily was sitting on the gray couch watching something on her phone. I was disappointed she hadn't shown more interest in the boxes. At least the ones that contained her grandmother's letters and photographs. Lily was an intelligent and curious teenager. But the scope of what interested her had steadily grown smaller as she got older.

After breakfast, I carried the boxes of correspondence and paperwork upstairs to my office and stacked them on the floor beneath my desk. Then I found room for the boxes of photographs in the dining room closet—after Paula moved three large containers of fabric into her office. Finally, I sat down on the living room carpet with a fresh cup of coffee and opened the first box of CDs.

My mother always had music playing in her house. It was her escape and her joy. Mostly jazz she could hum along with in her warm alto voice while doing other things. She always heard the tune, found the melody, and joined in, seemingly without thinking about it.

I flipped through her discs of Sarah Vaughan and George Shearing, Ella Fitzgerald and Louie Armstrong, Miles Davis, Duke Ellington, and Bill Evans. I paused when I came to Count Basie and his Kansas

City Five. I opened the case and slipped the disc into the CD player, turned the volume down, and sat on the carpet not moving a muscle. Simple perfection flowed out of the speakers.

I continued flipping through the CDs until I saw Francis Wong's, *Ming.* The bright green and yellow lettering, purple-blue background and red Chinese characters jumped out at me like a miniature billboard extolling the benefits of wandering off in unexpected directions.

I studied the photo of Francis Wong: head bent forward, jaw set, sleeves rolled up. I turned the CD over and scanned the names of the tunes. There was no way this CD should be here, I mumbled to myself. I ejected Count Basie and inserted Frances Wong. His swirling rough-throated tenor saxophone, the thumping drums, and clattering bells, rushed out of the speakers. Ten seconds later Paula told me to turn it off. Too much for a Sunday morning, she complained.

I had seen Francis Wong perform a few times in the 1990s at a place called Radio Valencia, on the corner of Valencia and 23rd Street in San Francisco. A cross between a coffee house and a restaurant, with cheap food and drinks; red walls, dark wood, velvet curtains; a long row of windows and a raised stage in the back.

Francis Wong's playing was forceful and fervent. Overflowing with subtlety. He was part of a small group of young players trying to jumpstart the jazz scene in San Francisco. To make it real. Not something regurgitated for tourists.

Paula was right, *Ming* was too intense for Sunday morning, but I had heard something on that record that got inside my feelings and started to change them.

I must have given the CD to my mother, I decided. Although I couldn't imagine why. There had never been a time when she enjoyed that kind of jazz. Mom wanted music to be soothing and uplifting. Even Charles Mingus was too much for her. Then I realized it was much more likely that I had forgotten the CD at her house. And now I had found it again.

A few days passed before I had the house to myself. I closed the curtains, cleared off the couch, and put *Ming* back in the player. Francis Wong blasted out of the speakers like a sorcerer on the razor's edge of lyric beauty. His saxophone slashed through the air like a flaming sword. I lurched forward on the couch, fully alert, as if a supernatural presence had entered the room.

Since my mother's death, I had felt like I was locked inside a gray box and I didn't know how to get out. I had studied the photographs of my mother's house I had taken shortly before she died, with its chaotic colors and eclectic style—thinking that these images would force grief's hand. I had gazed at photos of her and my father, strolling on a Southern California boardwalk, or camping somewhere in the woods—hoping the reminder that she had once been young and happy and full of enthusiasm for the future would allow grief to flow. I had sifted through photos of my mother's childhood in Detroit, playing with her little brother, Edward, in front of their small wooden house on Burt Road, photos of her laughing with friends from her Catholic high school, or lounging in a park on the hood of someone's car—to remind myself that everything repeats, that there is no beginning or end, only ripples fading as they spread. I had told Paula all the stories I could remember my mother telling me, even though Paula had heard them all before—to see if something in her reaction would unblock the grief that I knew must be there. None of this helped in the slightest. Grief remained just a word. A possible side effect one might experience after the death of a parent.

This finally began to change that afternoon when I sat on the couch listening to Francis Wong. His music knocked the pictures off the wall of my inner lostness and revealed a hidden door and labyrinthian tunnel. Only then did my numbness turn into feeling. Only then did tears begin to fall.

The gray box had opened. I stepped out of it and into a stiff wind; a swift stream. To keep my balance, to give me hope of making it to the other side, I searched for more Asian Improv. I discovered musicians as different as Jon Jang and Fred Ho and Art Hirahara. They helped build the sonic scaffolding from which I could air my grief out like laundry on pull-lines in San Francisco backyards.

The jazz side of their music connected me to my mother, and my father, to what I already knew and loved, while the Asian side of the music led me to the edge of an unknown land. Every new record I heard pushed me a little closer to seeing something in my mother's death that I had felt but couldn't name. The feelings the music opened up in me had nothing to do with memory or regret. What I felt wasn't understanding or forgiveness. In the middle of not remembering and not forgetting, not hating and not loving, not getting stuck and not moving on, I began to see something like the dance of compassion take shape inside my head.

Then Bandcamp led me to Yusuke Ogawa's compilation series of Japanese jazz. And his comment in some liner notes, that listening is believing, became a kind of credo of mine. I fell in love with his collection of music celebrating Jiro Inagaki's 90th birthday. The more I listened to that record the more grief shaded into joy and joy became a long road arcing through an idea of Japan that led me to Chiura Obata's Yosemite and Albert Saijo's Heart Mountain.

The tenor and baritone saxophones got me part way there; the piano and electric guitar; the bass, the drums, bells and gongs, got me a little closer. But it was the sound of the human voice, of two women singing Cantonese pop songs on a Gary Lucas record called, "The Edge of Heaven," their voices achingly lovely, singing in a language that flickered and danced, infinitely subdividing grief, that finally showed me there was life inside my mother's death.

By the time Christmas rolled around, my obsession with Asian music had settled into something closer to medicinal. I didn't even have to enjoy what I was listening to for it to make me feel like it was cleansing my system and adding nutrients that would make me stronger in the future.

One evening, I was sitting in our living room that smelled of dog, with our old cat brushing against my leg, drinking a nice Scotch, and wishing my mother was there to enjoy it with me. Once again, I was sitting on our soft gray couch, in the sweet spot between the floor standing speakers, where the music had a warmth and immediacy, even at low volume, listening to a Korean group that mixed a traditional plucked instrument with electronics and pop vocals. I settled into the couch, with my legs outstretched, sipping the Scotch, anticipating the weary relaxation and quiet sadness I had almost come to enjoy, when something shifted inside my head.

Unexpectedly, I felt angry with my mother. It took me a few seconds to understand that I wasn't mad at her for dying. No. I was mad because I had let her donate her body to science. It felt wrong. Even if it made sense.

My mother never visited my father's grave, or her father's. She didn't go to her own mother's funeral or her brother's. She was in as much denial about other people's death as she was about her own. Even cremation was too much for her. It required planning ahead. And cost something. And someone would have to pick up the ashes and do something with them. Donating her body to science would be free, fast and without hassle. But it left me with nothing, not even an urn of ashes to forget about on the mantel.

After the music was over and my glass was empty, I felt agitated and unsure about what to do next. I sat frozen on the couch, halfway between standing up and sinking deeper into the cushions. Paula was upstairs in our bedroom talking on the phone to her mother in Germany. Lily was brushing her teeth with the electric toothbrush in the bathroom with the wavy blue tiles.

Lily was an energetic and healthy fourteen-year-old, but what if something happened to her? What if she got sick, or fell off a balcony, or tripped and fell in front of an oncoming car? What if she was snatched away from me? I sank deeper into the couch, feeling anxiety wash away my anger. There had to be something I could do for my child.

Sensing that I was heading into an emotional nose dive, I took a few deep breaths, and tried to calm myself down by thinking about something mundane, like what was on my to-do list for the next day. I loved to-do lists and had developed a complicated taxonomy of them on my phone, which I began to calmly flip through. It didn't help.

I thought about listening to more music and/or drinking more Scotch. That might help, a little. That's when I thought that maybe I should give my imagination a try. My imagination, which, at one time, had behaved like a well-trained dog, walking right at my side, impervious to squirrels and cats, other dogs, and other people, until I set it free, and it shot off in unexpected directions.

I lay down on the couch with my arms at my side. I closed my eyes and tried to create some space for my imagination to do its work. Drowsy from the Scotch and relaxed by the music, I couldn't fight off sleep for long and soon I began dreaming that I was in the audience of some kind of auditorium. The lights dimmed, a red and gold curtain glided open, a spotlight flicked on. A bald man with a long gray beard walked on stage. He sat down on a bar stool and started playing an electric guitar fashioned out of a beaten-up hard-shell suitcase. He sang a long-winded story-blues about a group of beings he called the League of Creative Embalmers, Toll-Takers and Dirge-a-Holics, who, as he sang it, existed outside of time, like working class angels, wandering the earth claiming souls according to arcane rules and mystical procedures.

When he finished the song and quietly walked off stage, nobody clapped, and nobody stood up. The spotlight spun around and found me in the audience, pining my frightened body to the seat. I woke with a start, instinctively covering my face with my hands.

I sprung up from the couch in a new panic. What's the matter with me? I'm probably the one who'll be next. Talk about denial! My head felt like it was held in a vice grip that might have been my own two hands pressing against my temples. There had to be something I could do for Lily, to make it easier for her once I was gone.

I lay back down on the couch and closed my eyes. It felt like a bag of sand had been dropped on my chest. My mind spiraled through a million images looking for one that would stop the free-fall. Finally, I found it. A plain pine box that could rest on two folding chairs at the foot of the bed. Something to fill with books and other objects that would provide advice and sustenance. Simple and symbolic. Ample in size. Flexible in design. Perfect for sharing a lifetime of wisdom and experience with those you love.

The relief lasted only a few seconds, however, before the obvious question popped into my head. What should I put inside that simple pine box? My mind went blank and stayed blank. I couldn't think of a single thing to leave for Lily. The bag on my chest grew heavier. I tried to wiggle out from under it, but I was pinned in place. Finally, after twisting left and twisting right, after summoning all the strength I could muster, the bag of sand slipped off my chest and fell with a thump on the floor in front of the couch.

I slowly stood up, patted my body and rubbed my head, then I slowly walked down the back stairs into the yard, feeling unsteady and short of breath. I muscled the water-logged cover off the hot tub, undressed, and climbed in.

A few months later, after a painfully slow drive home from the library in San Francisco where I worked, I stood on the back deck to decompress. Dusk was turning into night. The lush yards all around were becoming inky, almost watery, shadows. The cool air felt thick and moist. A few feet away, Paula sat in her office sewing little pouches out of bright sparkly fabric on a noisy commercial grade sewing machine. In the kitchen, Lily sat at the table doing homework. I could hear her punching the keys of a calculator and typing on her laptop.

Standing in the dim twilight, looking at the majestic trees growing along the creek, cutting through backyards, and crossing the busy street around the corner, my head suddenly fogged up and I felt displaced.

Seagulls circling over the trees scraped cymbals and saws with their drill-like beaks and skeleton-like claws. I thought I heard a piano repeating the evening news and the evening news and the evening news, getting louder and louder like the TV in my mother's living room, until it sounded like Norteño accordions played by gardeners and bricklayers, trying to steal back the soul of her California, of my California, where so many in our family ended up, refugees from failed Midwestern factory and farm towns.

I hurried back inside, turned on the oven and got a pizza out of the freezer. While the oven warmed up, I went into the living room and absentmindedly flipped through a box of my mother's LPs. What

I liked most about those records, especially the big band music from her youth, was their pure exuberance. The bright bustling beat of futuristic buzz-chasing optimism captured in those recordings sounded like an unstoppable force of nature.

I paused when I saw a Dave Brubeck record of Cole Porter tunes. Maybe a bit of local magic would make me feel better? Brubeck from Concord. Desmond from San Francisco. I put the record on the turntable. The sound of honey-light and serpentine rock poured out of the speakers, soothing everything inside of me that could be soothed.

We ate pizza and salad sitting around the scuffed up wooden table. Magenta bougainvillea blossoms nearly covered the window. Through them I could see the pinkish-white blooms of the tree-rose growing on the side of our old, detached garage. Spring rains had turned the backyard into a blooming jungle, just the way Paula liked it. But we were still in drought, and everything would be brittle-dry in a few months.

Paula asked if I would make miso salmon later that week, with a spinach salad. Her way of saying it was time for things to get back to normal. She was worried. She thought I was wandering around the edges of grief without really feeling it, distracted by strange music, and drinking too much. Paula's thick hair fell across her face as she leaned over to pick up the dishes. She had almost no gray. It wasn't fair. She was only a year younger than me, and I had been gray for at least a decade.

I watched Lily get her books out and return to her homework. She had my father's blond hair and my mother's long legs. She had my chin and Paula's eyes. Lily had been a kooky kid who liked to wear three or four colorful dresses, plus pants and a skirt, a hat and a scarf, all mixed up at the same time. Bright as a field of wildflowers. When did she become the kid who planned everything out in advance? Who did Thursday's homework on Monday. Who knew what outfit she was going to wear next Tuesday. Who told me on Wednesday what she wanted for lunch on Friday. Who kept lists of fun activities, of fun vacations, of fun restaurants. But who never asked me how I felt after my mother died. That kind of thing wasn't on any of her lists.

On my way to the bathroom, I glanced at the Brubeck album lying on the couch. On the cover was a photograph of a woman's long silky legs, from her thighs down to a pair of shiny gold slippers. The cover reminded me of photographs of my mother. Her long legs as she sat on a brick wall. Her long legs sunbathing. Her long legs running across the grass in a photograph I had scanned, printed, and put up on the wall as part of a makeshift memorial.

That photo was taken in 1964 when my mother would have been 31 or 32 years old. She was tall and thin, and her thick dark hair bounced behind her, pushed back by a plastic hair band. She was holding a can of Olympia beer, and there was a huge smile on her face as she flew toward the camera, arms held out stiffly and a little behind her, like wings.

That summer my friend Timmy announced he was going to drive out from Arizona to see me, because he was concerned about my state of mind. My first thought was that Paula must have called him. Then I figured he was just looking for an excuse to come to the Bay Area.

I met Timmy in college. He had moved to San Francisco from Minneapolis, via Mexico. San Francisco became our common ground. The city felt like a throwback to a different era. Fog-soaked, a little rundown, cramped, dirty, and still artistic. It was like living on an island off the coast of California.

Timmy left the Bay Area a few years later to get a Ph.D. in English Literature at Alabama, followed by a short adjunct teaching gig in Vermont, before landing a tenure track job in Tucson.

Timmy said he loved the southern border, that it was the most exciting place he had ever lived. San Francisco may be your ecstatic Beat poet, he liked to taunt me, but the border is my Shakespeare. Every day it writes a new tragedy, comedy, or history.

Timmy could really be an asshole, like most academics. But I was impressed that he had stuck it out and finished his Ph.D. Even if his immigrant parents would have preferred that he had gotten a master's degree in computer science or had gone to medical school. Nevertheless, he was a university professor, while I was merely an administrator in a university library.

You may get summers off, I goaded him, but you had to move to bum-fuck Arizona, whereas I got to stay in the Bay Area. Who got the short end of that stick?

I love Arizona and the heat and the border, Timmy answered with enough confidence that I felt like believing him.

A few days later he surprised me by saying he wanted to visit Chinatown. Timmy wasn't the type to seek out tourist attractions or kitschy destinations. What had gotten into him?

Did you know that Chinatown was built for tourists, not the people who lived there? Timmy asked, repeating something he had read in a book he found lying on the floor in Paula's office.

Chinese people may have been in San Francisco since day one, or at least since the Gold Rush, he went on, but it was some entrepreneurial white guys who decided to redecorate the neighborhood, to make it look more like the Chinese cities in popular postcards. They splashed some red paint around. Added a bunch of Chinese writing. Built some decorative balconies. And voila, exotic Chinatown was born.

The next day we drove over the sleek, elegantly minimal, new Bay Bridge, into ever new and ever improved San Francisco. As we drove, Timmy kept throwing facts at me from Paula's book.

Did you know, Timmy asked, as smugly as possible, that one time white San Franciscan's even built a wall around Chinatown, to turn it into a playground of opium dens and squalid whorehouses for tourists? What a bunch of assholes!

That sounds like bullshit to me, I told him. Maybe what you're reading is a novel?

Yeah, maybe, he admitted, but it doesn't sound all that far-fetched to me. Just more crazy white people history. Another example of the terrible shit they do, then try to pretend like it never happened.

If that's true, we're doomed. I moaned. If we can't count on San Francisco, what can we count on?

Timmy shrugged, opened his backpack, and took out a fancy camera. After making a few adjustments he started taking pictures through the car window. The new bridge. The small islands. The immense ships spread over the expansive bay waiting to dock in Oakland. Finally, he set the camera down in his lap.

Why do you think we're doomed, George?

I didn't answer him.

Don't be so dramatic, he went on, deciding to lecture me anyway. San Francisco will be fine. Even if we are living through an ugly kind of dark age.

I parked halfway up Russian Hill, and we walked down to Stockton Street. Every few seconds, Timmy stopped to take a picture. Not of a vista, or a beautiful building, but of an isolated detail, like the pattern of cracks in a square of sidewalk.

When I saw a sign for a place claiming to be the oldest temple in San Francisco, I dragged Timmy inside. On our way up the dilapidated wooden stairs we heard a Chinese ensemble practicing through a half-closed door. The stairs were wide and worn. A window opened onto a narrow air-shaft, filling the stairwell with light.

Timmy took pictures of individual stairs, of the railings and railing posts, of the windowsills and frames. I stood off to the side, listening to the music, which sounded like a Chinese chamber opera—intimate and theatrical.

I peered into the practice room and saw the musicians through the partially open door. The floor was rough wood, worn down to a faint grayish green. A large banner with red Chinese characters hung above a dark ornate table. An incense burner with three curling tails of smoke sat next to a carved figure of a woman.

The musicians were all men, mostly older, wearing regular clothes. But the singer was a beautiful young woman with long dark hair arranged like a crown on her head. She wore bright red lipstick and a long black dress with a turquoise dragon on the front. She waved one hand through the air as she sang, as if she were painting a story on a scroll of rice paper.

By that time, my interest in Asian music had faded almost completely. I still enjoyed listening to it, but it was no longer an emotional necessity. So, it was a surprise when I felt the singer's voice reach through my chest and grab my heart. I had to lean against the wall to catch my breath.

The formal, theatrical quality of her voice transmitted an understanding of death and mourning and nostalgia I hadn't found in my own culture. A sadness that was a tearing open and a healing. A strength that was delicate and light and razor sharp. I stood in the stairwell, transfixed, until one of the musicians got up and closed the door.

Later, when I tried to explain my reaction to Timmy, he responded dismissively.

Really? She was probably singing about lovely village rice fields in moonlight. Or about a young man who ran off to war and left her to mourn his spirit for eternity. Or . . .

I cut him off.

Come on, Timmy, the border separating two cultures can't be completely impermeable. The music crossed that border and touched me. That's all.

You can't just say *border* and think I'll let you off the hook. Timmy jabbed back. At least I speak Spanish. I know what the Mexican border singers are saying.

A few weeks after Timmy returned to Arizona, I had another memorable dream. In it, I was visiting my mother's small ranch-style house in Fresno. Modest as a matchbook from a cocktail lounge or bowling alley. I walked across the carport and knocked on the back door.

An old Chinese man wearing baggy gray pants and a loose-fitting t-shirt opened the door and silently welcomed me into the kitchen. Looking into his eyes made me want to visit ancient Chinese temples and to wander through modern Chinese cities that are said to be the cities of the future. The old man stood exactly where my mother's chipped white Formica table had been, with four heavy wooden chairs—blue, green, red and yellow—positioned around it. He slowly lowered his head, then called to a woman hidden in a nearby room.

Through the side window I saw the western redbud tree we had planted in the backyard as a memorial for my stepfather. Its bright leaves dancing with every subtle shift of breeze. I remembered Paula, Lily and I standing in a circle with my mother, sprinkling my stepfather's ashes around the roots of that tree.

My stepfather had a tree. A memorial tree with heart-shaped leaves that burst into pink flowers every spring. This man I could barely remember and who had tormented my mother with sickness and boredom for years had a tree. I looked back at the old man and asked, Where's my mother's tree?

Then the unseen woman spoke. Close the door. Tell him he doesn't live here anymore.

I remembered that dream question a few days later. *Where's my mother's tree?* While I stood at the sink, with the cool air from the open window fanning my face.

Each letter of each word in that question became a new face that looked like a face I had seen in my mother's photo albums, similar to my face, to my daughter's face, my mother's face, but different, and unsympathetic, and unforgiving.

But there is no tree. No urn of ashes. No gravestone. Science, wearing an old lab coat and surgical white mask, took what was left of my mother and quickly carried her out of our house, slid her into a van, and rushed her over the Bay Bridge into San Francisco.

When her body arrived, a bell rang, and a pair of doors opened. The elevator glided. Gurney wheels squeaked. Tissue samples were gathered, data points logged and analyzed.

Maybe a young medical student learned something new or gained a better understanding of something she had previously found vague and allusive.

So, what if she did.

Donating my mother's body to science was a mistake.

Memories need a place to gather,
a point to focus attention.
Stories need a stone to deface.

Chapter Seven

YOU ARE ALWAYS WELCOME

[mom]

I think I finally understand why I didn't like to travel as I got older. Because if you leave, you may never come back. You might get knocked off course, or sucked into someone else's life, or just get lost.

Whitey and I both had a wild hair when we were young. He was Mister Zig Zag; Mister To & Fro. I was Miss Further on Down the Road; Miss Always Keep the Past in the Rear-view Mirror.

When Whitey died suddenly on the side of the highway, I felt an alchemical transformation take place inside me. I don't mean the transformation of love and adventure into fear. I'm talking about every known thing getting small. Including my hopes, my dreams, my imagination. When I got over the shock, I felt like the itsy bitsy spider climbing out of the spout.

Now things feel big again. Well, that's not really true, because I'm talking about what the magazines used to call inner space, which never really has a size.

You still like to travel, George. You're retired. Got money in the bank. Can probably go anywhere you want. I'm starting to think that you're more into globe-trotting than trying to inch a little closer to your mother.

Guess you never figured out inner space either. All that talk about mind-trips and meditation and spiritual time travel, didn't help you in the slightest.

The mirror is turning.

Light bounces surface to surface.

Pulsing like a tune in search of its musical device.

It was still chilly that morning when I grabbed the newspaper from the driveway. The heavy robe I'd thrown over my pajamas, didn't help much. Why did I still subscribe to the *Bee,* I wonder, when it was all on the Internet? Habit, I guess. I liked sitting at the kitchen table with the gas heater going, while I read through the paper. It was comforting. Something I'd done all my life.

So, there I sat on a Sunday morning in that dead stretch between Thanksgiving and Christmas with the paper spread out in front of me on the table, my elbows planted in the middle of the page, totally stunned in an old person kind of way, when time twists in an unexpected direction and you're no longer sure where you are. Seeing Blondie and Peanuts cartoons in the paper through me for a loop. I mean, I remembered my dad laughing at Blondie, and he died in 1954.

I'd been thinking a lot about my dad since George took me to Detroit for my 60th high school reunion in June. I remembered how, when I was a little girl coming downstairs for breakfast, I'd usually find Daddy sitting at the kitchen table, leaning back in his chair, bobbing his head as he read the funny pages. Sometimes he'd laugh so hard the front legs of the chair would rock off the floor, like the chair itself had a sense of humor, or like it wanted to dance to the polka music wheezing out of the large boxy radio on the sideboard.

That was the house on Burt Road, near Rouge Park. A clapboard house, in a neighborhood of drafty wooden houses. Bedrooms up above; basement down below; the living room, kitchen, and dining room in between.

Daddy's laughter. Mommy's anger. Eddie's dramatics. My escape.

I must have mentioned the reunion to George right after the invitation arrived in the mail.

That's cool, you should go.

Maybe I will.

Come on, George said, hearing the hesitation in my voice. I'll go with you. You won't have to do anything except pack.

How could I say no after that?

That winter was mild, warmer, with less rain than normal. The sun was out more than it wasn't. One day followed another and I hardly felt the gloom that usually weighs me down in the winter months. Whenever George called to check in, he'd always bring the conversation around to Detroit. He wanted to make sure I understood how excited he was about going to Detroit and that it would be a big deal if I backed out.

By springtime, when my old roses had started to bud, and the Mexican gardener next door had begun mowing my grass again, Detroit started popping up in my dreams, like cartoons of childhood, not all of them very funny. I started to worry. It had been 60 years, after all. I had missed so many births and graduations and marriages and a long string of deaths. I hadn't even gone home when Daddy got sick, or even for his funeral after he died. What's the point of going back now? And for a high school reunion at that.

As June 3rd approached, I started to feel more and more trapped, like George had tricked me into saying I would go. One day, I stumbled and almost fell on the way to the bathroom. I told George that my doctor wouldn't let me travel. Too dangerous for a woman my age.

George didn't buy it. He booked the tickets and arranged for us to stay with my cousin Marylin in Detroit.

Don't think about the trip, he told me. When it's time, we'll just do it. George had an irritating habit of trying to make things sound simpler than they were. Both in the words he used and his tone of voice. Your 60th high school reunion? Sounds like fun. We'll see some of your old haunts, cruise around beautiful old, abandoned Detroit, eat some classic food, have a beer or two. It'll be easy-peasy.

Better not to respond to nonsense like that.

But, in a sense, George was right. The days flew by. Then, one evening, George was at my door, lugging his carry-on suitcase inside. I could tell he wanted to stay up and talk, but I was worried about having to get up so much earlier than I like, so I went to bed as soon as I could.

Next morning, I was dreaming that I was living in an old cabin by a lake, probably in the upper peninsula, tucked into a feather bed, when the alarm went off, and everything disappeared. I smelled coffee and heard George running the faucet in the kitchen. My head felt too heavy to lift. I rolled over and clung to the blankets. Slowly, my blood started flowing again, thoughts returned, the familiar shadows of my room edged me toward wakefulness.

Next thing I knew, George was pushing me through the airport in a wheelchair. When we got to our seats in the back of the plane, I finally accepted the fact that I was going back to Detroit. I had to admit that it felt good to get away. To break the spell of the same old same old. I thanked George and meant it.

It was only when we landed and it took forever to get off the plane, that I started to get nervous. There was another wheelchair waiting in the jet-way, but I said, no. I didn't want Marylin to see me in a wheelchair. We slowly walked down the ramp, pausing three or four times for me to gather energy, and to strengthen my resolve, before the flow of departing passengers pushed us into the chrome gleam, the arched ceilings, the non-stop noise, and bright daytime lights of the terminal. I glanced up and thought that George looked a little nervous too.

Here we go, he said under his breath, pointing at a woman holding a hand-painted cardboard sign.

Fresno Cuzz!!
Putsey [hand drawn flower]
Welcome!!!!

I almost froze when I saw that sign, I wanted to turn back, to put off seeing Marylin again. I told George that I needed to use the bathroom, but he ignored me and started to walk faster, pulling me along with him.

Putsey was Marylin's nickname for me. I don't have the faintest notion what it means or why she called me that. Somebody should write a book about nicknames. Where they come from. Why they stick. Why some people have one and others don't.

Good thing Marylin was holding that sign, though, or I don't think I would have recognized her. She had turned into a big woman, with short gray hair. A strange, unfamiliar woman. Until she spoke and her voice triggered a wave of recognition. Marylin and her brother Norvol had been my favorite cousins.

George insisted that I sit in the front seat of Marylin's car, and that he sit in back. He probably had his notebook on his lap, trying to write down everything we said. Or maybe he just stared out of the window soaking in the strangeness of Detroit.

I was a little uncomfortable. Wondering what Marylin was going to ask and what she was going to tell. But she played nice, sticking to questions about my family and working life. My house and garden. Questions about living in Fresno and whether I still liked California.

Let me see if I can fill you in on 60 years of family history in 30 minutes, Marylin kidded, as she pulled onto the freeway. You know my husband left us a few years ago, right? Just after Norvol. Thank God for my son and his little boy.

It's great being a grandmother, isn't it, I chimed in.

Marylin nodded and started running through all the cousins and aunts and uncles I could barely remember. One has a good job in Chicago. One has a daughter with a condition, something serious, but I forget what. One still lives at home. One has a new wife. One moved to Florida. One to Cleveland. One to Toronto. So many forks in the road. I got confused and felt happy in a smug kind of way that I'd gotten out and moved to California.

A few minutes later we pulled into Marylin's driveway. We walked through her living room and dining room and sat down in the kitchen. Marylin's house was homey in an old-fashioned familiar kind of way. Family photos, doilies, overstuffed chairs and couch, framed churchy images hanging on the walls. Clock radio, microwave, Mr. Coffee. Marylin certainly didn't go out of her way to express her individuality.

She warmed up some leftovers and offered us both a Bud Lite. I kept looking at Marylin's face, struck by its angelic glow. That's when it hit me. this wasn't another weired twist in time, I really was in Detroit. Exhausted. Confused. Feeling underwater from the travel and time difference. But here I was, back in Detroit for the first time in 60 years.

Next morning, I woke up to the sound of birds in the yard. I got out of bed and stretched a little to see how my back felt. Not too bad, given how soft the bed was. There were posters of sports stars on the wall. A Lego spaceship on the dresser. George had left my suitcase on a chair next to the closet. I unzipped it and pulled out a pair of loose-fitting jeans, a light-weight blue top with buttons halfway down the front, and a denim vest. I hung up the dress I was going to wear to the reunion, then slowly made my way to the kitchen.

George was sitting with Marylin at the breakfast table. The sunlight shining through the window was bright and watery. After pouring me some coffee, Marylin fried eggs and made toast for breakfast.

When she sat down, she said, now that you're finally here, what do you want to do?

George piped up that he wanted to see the old house on Burt Road, which he'd found on the Internet, and that he also wanted to go to Dodo's house on Northlawn.

Okey-dokey, Marylin responded. Want to go to the cemetery too?

Marylin's kitchen was a beige almost brown color, with white tile counter-tops. American flags, Catholic saints, and virgin Mary's lurked in nooks and crannies, on the calendar and fridge magnets. For some reason, they didn't bother me the way they usually did. She filled our coffee cups and cleared the table. When she sat back down, her expression had changed.

Forgive me if this sounds like a strange question, Georgie, but how do you feel about psychics? I stared at her, but didn't know what to say. She explained that last year she'd gone to a psychic who predicted that a favorite relative of hers, who lives far away, was going to visit her soon. That was way before I knew you were coming, she added. And here you are sitting in my kitchen.

I've had my horoscope done a few times, mostly just for the fun of it. And maybe my palms read, but I don't think I've ever gone to a psychic, I told Marylin, feeling a little uncomfortable with her question.

Marylin calmly added more sugar to her coffee, then she told me that Dodo had also been a psychic. Dodo was my grandmother. She kept Tarot cards in the living room cabinet, Marylin explained, which she brought out whenever someone asked for her help.

I was so sure that Marylin was making up this business about Dodo being a psychic, that I started to shake my head, ready to dismiss the whole thing. Dodo's house had been neat and proper. No beads or incense. No unusual books. No gatherings. Then a dim memory floated to the surface. Dodo wearing a dark house dress, sitting at her dining room table with the lights off, candles burning, spreading a deck of colorful cards out in front of her. A young woman sat across the table, obviously upset.

I don't remember what I thought Dodo was doing at the time. Or what I thought telling someone's fortune really meant. When I got older, I didn't take any of that stuff seriously. It was just a scam or a party trick. But I didn't take dying seriously either. And, well, now I know it doesn't matter what you think. What happens happens and then you adjust.

What about you? I asked Marylin.
Nope. I didn't get the gift.
And my mom?
I don't think so.
And your mom, Etta?
Oh, for sure, she was always reading tea leaves and people's palms. She really believed in all that stuff, even though she was a good Catholic.

That clicked. Etta had had wild hair and her eyes darted around in her head like she was looking for a way into your thoughts. My mother's older sister was fun to be around. She laughed a lot and made jokes at Mom's expense.

While Marylin cleaned up, George and I stepped outside and waited on the back porch. The air was lush and vibrant. It had been a long time since I'd felt the electricity of summer.

At the end of the driveway, sat the garage. Fresh white like Marylin's house. Lawn thick and green. Bright purple flowers along the fence. Marylin came out jingling her car keys.

Hang tight while I get the car. She opened the garage door. An old yellow VW Bug, put halfway back together, sat tucked away in the corner. Marylin got into her plain Jane sedan and backed it out of the garage. We got in.

It looked like every house on the block had an identically shaped lawn, painted the exact same shade of green. With mighty trees arching over the street. Perfectly lovely. Summer is the life season in Detroit. Not like Fresno.

George guided Marylin to Burt Road, which was rough and full of holes. It had been patched up so many times it looked like a jigsaw puzzle. A lot of the houses in the old neighborhood were rundown or abandoned with junk scattered on lawns so green they looked artificial—a voracious green you never see in California.

It didn't seem possible that our shaky old house on Burt Road would still be standing. But it was. Just like George said. With a fresh coat of white paint and a black bistro table out front with a plant in a white pot sitting on it.

I studied the house. Same windows; new dark gray trim. Same drainpipe; different shaped hedge. Same concrete steps; same concrete walkway; different century.

George asked Marylin to take a picture of the two of us. Then he sheepishly mentioned that Paula thought we should knock on the door and ask if we could take a look inside.

I stepped toward the door, then stopped.

You do it.

George shook his head and didn't move.

Just then another memory rushed forward and distracted me from commenting on George's wishy-washy behavior.

I'm a young girl eating toast in the kitchen. Daddy walks down the stairs and steps into the dining room, wearing a dark blue suit with a yellow bow tie and a wonderful bowler hat, shiny black shoes, and dazzling white spats, looking like the proud owner of something everybody in the neighborhood wants, but only he has. It must have been the weekend. Weekdays Daddy wore work clothes. Dark shirts, overalls, heavy boots. With his bulbous red nose and sparkling blue eyes he reminded me of President Roosevelt crossed with W.C. Fields.

What's got you strutting around like a rooster? Mother snapped, blocking his way to the table.

The new Krazy Kat cartoon, he chuckled. I want to show it to Georgiana.

Not so quick, Mr. Bigshot. First, she's got to mop the kitchen floor, and bake some bread, and weed my roses, and clean sweet Eddie's butt. That's how it felt anyway, standing in the front yard, 60 years later. Like I had been the poor stepdaughter, and my mother the strict stepmother, and Daddy the clueless old man who tried to make us all happy.

Standing in front of my old house, it was the front door, which the new owners had, for some mysterious reason, painted black, that sucked me in. On the other side, Daddy lived to be 100. And I wasn't old. And my life was not almost over. The twinkle in Daddy's eye reassured me of that. I imagined him waltzing with the wind. An opera of laughter and love emanating from his fading body.

It still doesn't seem right that mother was the performer when my parents met. She was a chorus dancer at the Capitol Theater. Daddy was just the electrician, making sure the girls got their moment in the spotlight.

Why she hated him I never understood. Without Daddy there would have been no laughter in our house. Of course, he did get her pregnant at 17 when he was 30 something. Knocked her life on to a completely different track.

Would I hate any man who got me pregnant at that age? Hard to say. At least he stuck with her. Gave her two kids. And this sweet little house on Burt Road.

The chrome door handle caught the light and I became aware of how heavy and sad I felt. I wiped a few tears from my cheek, clutching a disposable film camera in my other hand.

What are we doing here, George? This house doesn't mean anything to you.

Of course, it means something, George countered. It feels special, somehow. George added a second later, his smile working overtime.

Why?

I can't quite put it into words.

Convenient, I thought. I bet you just enjoy posing your mother like she's the subject of a low-budget documentary. Stand right here, under the street sign, look at your old house. What thoughts are you thinking? What feelings are you feeling? What memories are swelling to the surface?

If George had really asked me any of those questions, I would have sent him on a long walk around the block, like he was still a little boy I could tell to go play with his friends until it got dark.

Even then, it was getting harder and harder for me to deal with time. The layers of the past and angles of the present pressed against each other, forcing this edge up, that one down, raising a mountain here, collapsing a valley there. Going anywhere was a challenge. Better to stay put if you could manage it.

George got us back in the car. He told Marylin to turn right on Joy Road. The fortified liquor stores, run-down auto parts shops, the laundromats, and fast-food stops, all looked small and temporary, like stage props, or something a kid made with blocks. Shrinking beige facades rolled by, vague industrial blue and chemical yellow walls blurred together.

Staring through the windshield, I kept asking myself, is this all Detroit is now? A few strokes of ink, some quickly drawn shapes, a wisp of a hint of a sad old joke, frame after frame.

Marylin kept up the friendly chatter while she drove. What a pleasant surprise to see how nice the house on Burt Road looked, she commented. I didn't expect that. My son just painted his house, he has a lovely room waiting for me when I'm ready to sell and move in with him.

George asked if she followed the Lions or the Tigers. Marylin said she didn't care for baseball or football. Hockey was her sport. And, she was rather proud to inform us, she was still on a team that played once or twice a week. Her teammates were fun women who liked to lock sticks, body check, and drink a few beers after the game. I kept sneaking a glance, to see if this overweight woman in her 70s was pulling my leg.

We turned left on Oakman and right on West-field, and there was Grandma Dodo's house on the corner of Northlawn, looking neat and trim, like it always had. The same two-toned brick walls, white awning out front, side yard with ancient roses.

Hey, I told George, I remember those roses from when I was a little girl.

He gave me a skeptical look.

What do you know about roses, I demanded.

Marylin swung the car around and parked in front of Dodo's house. That's another nickname I just accepted without wondering where it came from.

Dodo? What, like the extinct bird? My grand-mother's real name was Henrietta, like Marylin's mom. Two Henrietta's. Guess that's why one of them needed a nickname. We got out and walked up to the corner.

While George asked Marylin questions about what the neighborhood had been like when she was a kid, I stared at Dodo's familiar brick house, where it seemed I had spent every holiday and every birthday when I was young. I guided my memory past all the normal conversations at normal meals, all the normal problems and normal solutions, to the moment when the drapes were drawn, candles lit, and the tarot cards were spread across the dining room table.

The Juggler, the Magician, the Female Pope. The Lovers, the Hermit, the Wheel of Fortune. The meaning of the cards never revealed themselves to me. There was no electric tension in the air. I waited and waited and when I couldn't even make up a good story about Dodo the Fortune Teller in my head, I gave up.

Now, of course, I wish I had a better appreciation for the arcana of life. Somehow, I missed that part of childhood. When you learn that living is magic.

The front door opened and a Black woman with her young son stepped onto the porch. She looked at us quizzically.

Not for sale, folks. Just in case you're wondering.

George stepped forward and said, I'm sorry, we're just taking a quick look, my mother's grandmother used to live here. We're visiting from California.

Your mother's grandmother? That's going back some. Does the house look the same? She asked walking toward us. George turned to me.

Exactly the same, I answered her.

You thinking of moving back to Detroit?

Oh, God no! I said. Almost spitting in my excitement to set her straight.

She smiled and guided her son past us. Didn't think so. But Detroit's not all bad. And you should never let fear stop you from doing something you really want to do.

Damn wise woman. Getting under my skin like that. Needling me with her smiling words. But she was right. I was afraid of Detroit. Afraid of the reunion, afraid of seeing Dodo's house, and the Burt Road house, too. I was afraid of the drive back to

Marylin's, and the nap I needed before the reunion, and the clothes I'd brought to wear. I was afraid of the hotel, the old women who were teenagers the last time I saw them. I was afraid of the talking and listening and seeing—and thinking about it all afterwards.

George dropped me off at the front door of the huge hotel where the Our Lady of Mercy reunion was being held, then found a spot in the parking lot. The lobby was sparkling and noisy. There was a sign telling us to take the elevator to the 2nd floor. A young woman wearing a Detroit Lions t-shirt handed us our name-tags and directed us down the hallway. The gray carpet, with its busy diagonal patterns, nearly gave me vertigo. I grabbed George's arm and stared straight ahead.

I knew it. My flowery burgundy dress felt too California the minute I stepped into the small banquet room and saw what the other women were wearing—a mix of stuffy formal and fluffy casual. At least the double strand of pearls I was wearing fit right in. They were the one nice thing I had from my mother.

George mumbled that he was overdressed in his dark coat and bright tie, but I thought he looked great. And he wasn't the only son or grandson who had dressed up.

We took our seats at one of the round tables set-up in the room and introduced ourselves to the two women already sitting there. The first woman had a long thick face and frizzy gray-brown hair that fluttered in the AC. The other woman was puffy and overweight. They said their names and smiled. I scrutinized their faces for a hint of the girls they might have been. We exchanged names of the teachers we'd had and the girls we'd been friends with. I shook my head and sighed. Just my luck to have to sit with two women who appeared to be complete strangers.

They boasted that they had stayed friends all these years. And that they were next-door neighbors in a suburb north of Detroit. I kept repeating their names in my head, but it didn't help. They didn't remember me, either. To make things worse, they had never even visited California.

The conversation fizzled out once dinner was served. I moved my food around on my plate to make it look like I was eating. Pasta of some sort. Chicken in white sauce. Mushy vegetables.

George was getting nervous and restless. I'm not sure what he expected, but he seemed disappointed. On his way back from the bathroom, he picked up a program from the table by the door.

Guess how many of your classmates are here? He asked once he sat back down.

I don't know, 20?

Not even close. Just eight.

You're kidding! Eight? Really? They should have sat us all at one table so we could have stared at each other in disbelief.

The two women tittered nervously.

George started reading the names from the program, pausing after each one to check my reaction. With each name I felt more adrift. Who are these women? Did I ever know them? Did they ever know me? The last name on the list changed all that. Hildegard Zielinski. I scanned the room, checking the faces.

At the third table I thought, maybe. Maybe that petite woman with long flowing hair and big glasses, wearing a silver necklace, is Hildegard Zielinski. She noticed me looking, smiled back, and waved.

Moments later she was standing at our table.

Georgie?

Hilde?

I stood up and we hugged and I felt something old and cozy rise up inside of me. I remembered walking to Hilde's house in the Polish neighborhood nearly every morning so we could take the bus to school together. From Catholic grammar school all the way through Catholic high school. We were two light-hearted girls not overly concerned with hell or heaven. Goof-offs with decent grades. Sporty types. Me basketball, Hilde tennis.

You're not still in Detroit, are you? I cautiously asked.

Oh no, we've been in Sedona, Arizona, for years.

You've been to Sedona, haven't you? I turned to George.

Then I remembered how dismissive he had been. Sedona? George had frowned. Nothing more than a

New Age tourist trap for people who like paintings of red rocks and Native American art made in China.

I panicked that George was going to say something like that to Hilde. But he didn't. George could control his tongue much better than I ever could. Fortunately, he seemed mesmerized by this figure from my distant past. This piece of history come alive.

Hildegard Zielinski radiated warmth and goodwill. Hildegard Zielinski had a guest room with a view of Sugarloaf Mountain. Hildegard Zielinski made me feel like sixty years was nothing.

Hilde and George made small talk while I soaked up her presence. If I wore a hearing aid, I would have turned it off. No sounds, just Hilde's deep blue eyes, large and lake-like. Her fine eyelashes. Her soft forehead. Her tight curls, blondish silver, falling over her shoulders.

You and your son should visit. Really, Georgie. It's such a short flight from Fresno. You'd love Sedona.

I promised Hilde that I'd visit her in Sedona, and soon. She glowed.

You know you are always welcome, Georgiana Helen Mary Allen. You can stay as long as you like.

But we never did visit Hildegard in Sedona, did we George? What happened? Did I melt in the heat that summer when it reached 110, even 115 degrees? Did you quietly stop suggesting we go to Sedona because Detroit had worn you out? Or did you just get swept along in your life—volleyball for Lily, another trip to Germa-

ny to visit Paula's mom, some big project at the library. Probably all of the above, as per usual.

Oh well. I'm glad you took me to Detroit. Glad you checked that off your list. You must have gotten something out of it.

For me, going back to Detroit was kind of like trying to re-read a book with most of the pages torn out. Parts of it are interesting, and you can almost remember some of the missing chapters, but it's hard to follow, and you're not sure it's worth the effort.

Kind of like this game of Marco Polo I like to think we're playing. Trying to tag each other. And trying to avoid being tagged. No longer calling out single words.

—Marco.

—Polo.

Now we're spewing page after page of words into the air. No wonder we haven't found the right wavelength.

Besides, you're still breathing air and striving for success. While I'm trying to figure out how to breathe under water. If only we were amphibious, comfortable in water and air, moving seamlessly between the realms, like particles of loving light.

Chapter Eight

UNEXPECTED TREMORS IN MY HEAD

[son]

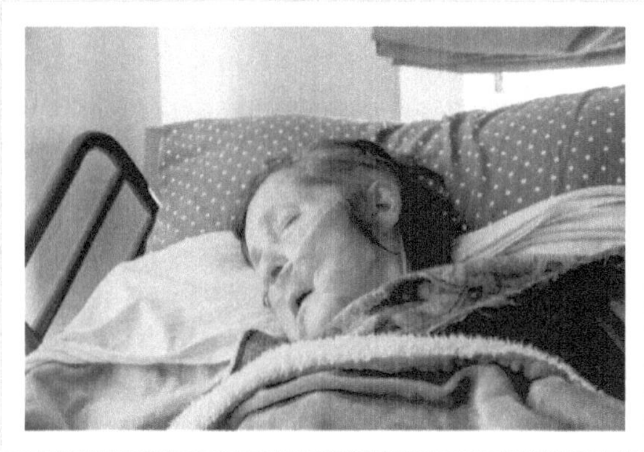

Driving down San Pablo Avenue to pick up a light bulb and some batteries at the hardware store, I heard a story on the radio that set off a series of unexpected tremors in my head. A movie director was talking about his latest movie in a pleasant, easy-going voice, when he abruptly changed topics, and said: I love it when I get visited by someone from the other side. I wish it happened more often. But when it does, I always feel like they have come to help me.

This comment didn't have anything to do with his latest movie, it was simply a way for him to express his interest in the supernatural. To show that for him otherworldly experiences were common enough to be mundane.

While signaling to change lanes to get around an AC Transit bus stopped at the curb, I glanced in my side mirror at the drivers speeding by. Have they all had otherworldly experiences? I didn't think so.

The glib movie director was selling pure nonsense. Not only did he have a house in Malibu, with a four-car garage and a bedroom-sized closet, but he also wanted us to think that he was so open and intuitive that helpful spirits dropped by to guide and entertain him.

He was trying to sound like Beatrix Potter discussing her intelligent encounters with animals. That was a novel, asshole, I grumbled. Not your made-up oversized life.

It was November 21st. A week before Thanksgiving, the 4th anniversary of my mother's death, and two days before what would have been her 88th birthday.

I slowed down. The traffic streamed by. Did all of these people believe in life after death, in the soul that continues after the body turns to dust? Wouldn't it be a different kind of world if they did?

I reached over to change the radio station, but for some reason I stopped myself. Instead, I swung into a parking space and turned the radio up. Just then, the interviewer brought the conversation back to the director's recent film and my mind began to wander.

I was starting to feel like the only human on earth who had never had any contact with what the director called *the other side*, when I remembered the incident at the abandoned baseball field. Grandfather George and Uncle Ed and the rest of the family were suddenly 100% there. Super real. Surrounding me with light-hearted love.

What about that?

Wasn't that the proof I'd been hoping for?

For a while, it felt like it was. Something monumental and life changing had been revealed. Giddy euphoria washed over me. Grandfather George and Uncle Ed had materialized from the other side to comfort me. Don't worry, their presence suggested, your mother will be with us soon. You'll see. There are other dimensions to this thing we call life.

A few weeks went by, then a few months. Then a few years. And nothing else happened. No contact whatsoever. Not from my mother, or my uncle or my grandfather, or any of the hundreds of other people who form the chain of consciousness that is my family.

When the radio host said it's time for a break, I noticed that I'd parked in front of the Albany Tap Room. I got out of the car. It was strangely warm for late November, a time of year when you used to be able to count on rain and harsh wind. Now it felt like any kind of weather could happen any time of year.

Football was on the big screen. People were drinking beer and eating. I sat at a round table near the door. The beer list was long and complicated. Clever names followed by short texts stating where the beer was brewed, followed by a flowery description of the flavor profile, and a set of numbers indicating alcohol and bitterness levels. The description of an IPA called Ravity's Grainbow got my attention:

Stuck between the world of science & speculative metaphysics? Sometimes all you need is a quaffable IPA to forget about the impending V-2 rocket strike.

I pulled my notebook and noise canceling headphones out of my backpack, feeling a little self-conscious. How many 61-year-old men carry Moleskin notebooks around with them?

What a pretentious old shit, I imagined the football fans at the next table thinking. Tuning us out and not even watching the game. Noting my silver-gray hair shaved fashionably short, my well-groomed goatee, my black sweater, expensive jeans, and designer glasses. And they were right. I was tuning them out, but just their overheated voices.

I liked watching them and I liked watching the game. I liked sitting in the bar. I liked sipping my beer. Because this was exactly the kind of place I would have gone to with my mother to celebrate her birthday. She didn't like football, but she loved people and the unpredictability of public spaces.

I raised my glass and toasted the air in her honor. I took another sip and watched a running play that resulted in absolutely no gain. Then I opened my notebook and started writing about my mother. This was something that Paula had encouraged me to. To help process my grief. And to capture memories of my mother for Lily before they faded away. I wrote:

Every day between 4 and 5 p.m. my mother would get a beer from the refrigerator and a glass from the cabinet. She would pop the top off the beer and pour it into the glass and take the first sip while standing in the kitchen. Then her whole body would relax, her face would flush, and she'd say: The best beer of the day!

After that, she'd put the open beer bottle back in the fridge with the bent bottle cap pressed over the mouth and carry her glass to the living room or the back porch.

Getting to the Best Beer of the Day was an achievement not to be taken lightly. The taste was so fresh, and the associations so rich. Proof she was still a woman who could experience the good things in life.

My mother's favorite beer was Heineken. An IPA like Ravity's Grainbow would have put her off. I laughed to myself, remembering the time we stopped at Sequoia Brewing on Olive. Once again football was on the screens. We sat at a rough-hewn wooden table. My mother wiggled out of her creamy white sweater and tried to get comfortable on the hard chair. Pictures of the Sierra Nevada mountains filled the wall near our table. An old logging saw hung next to the door, paraphernalia from the Fresno State Bulldogs football team was scattered around the room.

Mom said, pick something out for me. She didn't want to put on her glasses and strain to read the menu in the dim light. Let's try something a little different, she added.

When our beers arrived, we toasted, then took a sip. I almost choked. Mom spit her mouthful of beer out on the table and screamed, God damn it! What's in this fucking beer!

The waiter—a 30 something sporting a long, pampered beard—rushed over with a towel and a quizzical look on his face.

You okay? You know you ordered the chili pepper beer, right? You read the menu, right?

Of course, he was right. But he really should have warned us.

I zipped up my backpack and was about to walk out of the Albany Taproom, when I changed my mind and decided to order some fries, because I'd just thought of one more thing I wanted to write about my mom before I left.

Appetite of a Bird: My mother was a preemie. Four pounds plus a few ounces at birth. Her mother, a petite 17-year-old farm girl, who had moved to Detroit to earn some money, was probably glad to get the baby out of her womb early, while it was still small enough not to do too much damage. My mother was immediately put in an incubator, to keep her warm and safe, until she was strong enough to go home. She claimed that she had the appetite of a bird because she was a preemie. That something failed to develop properly in her digestive system.

I was in my late 30s before I noticed my mother didn't eat very much. Americans waste a lot of food. In that sense, my mother became more and more of an American the older she got. At home she mastered the art of cooking for one. She'd have a piece of toast, maybe some sweet yogurt and a bite or two of fruit for breakfast. Half a bologna sandwich for lunch. Some crackers and cheese with the first beer of the day. A can of soup for dinner, which she'd eat while watching the evening news or Jeopardy or a crime show like CSI.

When we went out to a restaurant, she never ate more than a corner of what she ordered. It didn't matter if it was a salad, a turkey sandwich, a taco, or a plate of pasta. When she was at our house it was even worse, especially at big meals like Thanksgiving or Christmas. She loved the smell of the turkey or Swedish meatballs cooking, the sizzle of bacon frying for the Brussels sprouts, the bubbling cranberries. She loved the look of a full plate of food. It was a necessary part of the holiday decorations, like the pine-cones on the windowsill and the long-tapered candles in the silver holders. But that didn't mean she needed to eat it.

I had to check whether incubators were in use in 1931. They were and had been for decades. But it hadn't been an easy sell. Many doctors felt like it didn't make sense to invest in preemie care because so many of the babies were going to die anyway.

At the 1896 World's Fair in Berlin, a German doctor noticed crowds of people lining up to see preemies displayed in tiny warming machines with windows. He realized that these curious, gawking, paying crowds, could save a lot of little lives.

In 1903 the German doctor opened a new attraction at Coney Island's Luna Park. Babies in incubators, tended to by pretty nurses. The barkers hyped the miracle cure and the money poured in.

I wish I had had the curiosity to look this up while my mother was still alive. I could have said: maybe you were a side-

show attraction. And she could have laughed at the thought that it might have been true.

My phone rang a few days later while I was standing in the makeshift pet cemetery and memorial corner of our backyard watering Paula's roses. My cousin Nancy had a favor to ask. Would I give her my Ancestry login so she could research her mother's side of the family.

A month or so earlier I'd sent her what I could find about her dad. It wasn't much. At least not much that we didn't know already. Edward Delano Allen, born January 19th, 1937, Detroit Michigan. Died February 8th, 2015, Port Charlotte, Florida. A bunch of marriages and children in between. Including Nancy's mother in 1962.

It's kind of silly what they try to pass off as meaningful information, I warned Nancy. No matter how many facts and figures they feed you, the mystery of a person always escapes the data.

She understood all of this, but she still wanted my password. You never know, she explained. A stray fact might unlock an old mystery. A chunk of gold might be found in a river of silt.

Go for it, I teased her. Nancy thanked me then lingered on the phone. So, Cuz, the reason I'm asking is that I just finished taking an on-line mediumship class and this old Black man kept appearing to me during the sessions. I'm sure we're related. Any Black people on your side of the family?

This is classic Nancy. She doesn't need science to confirm the fact that there is a Black man in her family tree, reaching out to her from the other side, but she hopes that science can tell her what his name is.

I was ready to hang up, but Nancy continued talking about her class. The social dynamics. The intrigue with the teacher. The breakthroughs while doing a psychic reading with another student.

I was having a hard time processing this new information. Nancy was already a professional astrologer and tarot card reader. She was a certified herbalist and she had recently finished a master's degree in Emotional Intelligence. Now she was becoming a psychic medium? My mind turned inside out. How can you train for something like that? You either have the gift or you don't, I thought.

I told Nancy about my experience at the abandoned baseball field. She accepted it without question. Like it was no big deal. When I explained that it was the one and only time I had experienced anything like that, she joked: Maybe you're just a late bloomer.

After getting off the phone, I walked upstairs to my office and noticed a small photograph taped to the wall above my desk of Nancy and me when we were young children, taken outside my mother's house in Fresno. Edward was sitting behind the wheel of a red Thunderbird convertible, smiling at the camera. Dark hair, olive complexion, looking like a model calmly waiting for someone to take his picture before he opened the car door and stepped onto the street.

Nancy was sitting on the hood. A round-faced kid with a monkish haircut, severe bangs, and big eyes. She looked like she was about three years old. I was standing next to her. Skinny, tall, and distracted.

I wished I could remember what I thought about Nancy back then. Like I wished I could remember what I thought about Edward and his shiny red car. But nothing surfaced. The same was true about most of my childhood. I remembered events and places but not what I was thinking or feeling at the time. Not even when I sat with stacks of family photographs. Or later when I sat zazen on a cushion staring at the light feathery-gray blinds.

I woke up my computer and looked at my mother's family tree. It only took a few inches to display four generations of mothers and fathers on my screen. The nodes progressed like stairs moving steadily into the past. It appeared so orderly. The kind of math a child would be comfortable with. Yet, if you added the siblings and children of siblings and eventual spouses and their parents and siblings and children and spouses and children it would be impossible to visualize the result as anything other than a tangled mess. The straight forward lines following mothers and fathers back in time were a fairytale.

Ancestry.com wants me to believe that they can contextualize my family story in relation to the bigger story of history. I'm hopeful, but most of the time I think it's bullshit. Their bots are not storytellers or poets or anthropologists.

I click on My DNA Story. According to the science, I am:

44% - English

27% - Irish

21% - Scottish

05% - Welsh

So, *my story* is 97% British Isles. Imbued with the swirling mists and vibrant green hills of travel poster landscapes, where my people were both the invaders and the invaded, the Celts and the Christians, the folklorists, and the believers in fairies. It's such an enticing story. But it's also frightening. The past feels a lot more infinite than the future.

I closed the computer and walked downstairs. Paula was watching a German police drama in the living room. Lily was at volleyball practice. It had been a weird November. White roses were still blooming in the yard and orange roses on the deck. The tomatoes and sage and rosemary and mint were still going strong. And a fresh blush of pink roses had just appeared on the garage.

It was warm enough to sit on the deck without a coat in the evening. Warm enough to remember the fires that never end. And that Nancy was living in a tiny house on a hilltop in Sonoma County. Two large fires burning nearby. I thought she'd be fine. She'd been dodging disasters for a long time. It was a dance she'd gotten very good at.

One afternoon, a few weeks later, I felt a surge of nervous energy that chased me out of the house and into the backyard. I sat down in an Adirondack chair, shaded by the Meyer lemon tree, and rested my laptop on a folding wooden table. That afternoon I decided to tell Lily how my mother didn't smile for 20 years.

Through the 1970s my mother beamed. A gap-toothed woman with large white teeth. Life was finally good again. She'd clawed herself out of the maw of depression. The 60s were a good decade to get your shit together, if you were open to it. Still, she was a single mother, working for sexist bosses.

Then just as she was starting to feel comfortable again, married for a second time to a man who promised a simple, stable life, I discovered my own escape trajectory through drugs and rock 'n' roll. Just when she thought her life had moved into the comfortable slow lane. That really pissed her off.

But I didn't steal her smile away. Mother nature in the form of gum disease and rotten teeth did the trick. Fear of dentists and lack of funds did the trick. At some point in the 1980s her lips clamped down, her self-consciousness took over, and there was only a ripple of a lip-smile to be seen.

In picture after picture, she's forcing herself not to smile, while trying to look happy. There she is at my university graduation. I'm in my purple cap and gown. Her arm threaded through mine, her bright eyes beaming at the camera. Her lips zippered shut.

My mother got dentures, just before Lily was born. Her smile came back, but it was different. Stiffer, more ridged. A ceramic smile. The line of her jaw also changed. The dentures had uncomfortable angles and planes and her mouth had to adjust to a new reality.

I closed my laptop and wandered around the backyard to clear my head. The Meyer lemon tree was full of plumb-size, greenish-yellow lemons, and one of Paula's roses was still blooming, with mottled orange flowers, tight as fists.

It was early December, but it smelled like a season that didn't exist. Between summer and a warmer autumn that was bright as a spring-like winter. Fresno had experienced more than 10 consecutive days over 115 degrees that summer. Fortunately, my mother didn't have to live through that particular end of the world.

I remembered how, as my mother's smile went through its metamorphosis, she became a motor mouth who couldn't stop talking. I sat back down in the Adirondack chair, woke my laptop up and started writing another entry for Lily.

As her second husband got sicker and sicker over the years, also from congestive heart failure, and failure to take his medicine, and listen to his doctors, he became a large silent presence slowly moving around the house. Not that different from one of her cats.

As if to compensate for his silence, my mother became the kind of person who didn't know what she thought or felt until she said it out loud. She would talk to herself, and she would respond to herself talking to herself.

She'd snap, that's utter bullshit, Georgiana!

Or she'd say, that's interesting, maybe you're on to something, old gal.

She was both the one speaking and the one listening to someone speaking, and without that bifurcation she couldn't decide what to eat for dinner, much less what she wanted to do with her body after she died.

At some point, her chattering became more like a twitch or a nervous tick, something she was no longer aware of doing.

When I visited, I would often get out of bed first. Brew some coffee. Pick up the newspaper from the driveway, and wait until I heard her voice, muffled but distinct, starting from her bedroom or bathroom, then getting louder as she shuffled up the hallway, passed my old bedroom, and inched into the kitchen.

Let's open the blinds and see if Whiskers and Frankie (her cats) want to come in.

What a yucky morning. Gray again.

That rose is finished. The grass in back is brown.

Why am I still paying those damn gardeners to come over?

There's that stupid mockingbird again.

Do I smell coffee?

The more she talked to herself the more embarrassed for her I felt. It was a sure sign that she was losing her mind. Then, at some point, I got used to it, and I started to like hearing her voice and not having to respond, or even think about what she was saying.

It was a kind of babbling song. The wind in the trees. Crickets in the yard. Traffic on West Ave. Until things turned dark.

God Damned Mexicans! She'd fume. They're always blasting their stupid um-pa-pa music. If they can't behave like real American, they should go home! Or she'd rant about the *city government not doing its job. All the potholes and garbage piling up. She'd rant about immigrants overrunning California. Africans and Muslims too. She'd rant about being scared in her own house. About drug overdoses and gunshots and loud cars racing up and down the street.*

She swore she was still liberal and always voted democrat. I wasn't so sure.

The older I get the more I pay attention to time. Not just the passing of time, but the variety of its shapes and forms. Time feels like the Milky Way, arching over my head, farther away than I can ever imagine. And, simultaneously, time feels like something I am trapped inside of, like a room, or a box.

The problem is you think time is real. I read that in a novel about a Buddhist temple sweeper. In that book, the past, present, and future are bound in a spiraling helix. Birth and death are brief flashes of light. What we call life nothing more than a scattering of words on a page that shine, then fade, then reappear in a different language waiting to be translated.

A few days after Thanksgiving, Nancy texted me. I was sitting at my desk, gazing at the clear blue sky, frustrated because Paula didn't want me to put bookshelves in our bedroom.

Bad news. Surgery. 9am tomorrow. Colon tumor removal. Yup. Will keep u posted.

When the test results came back positive, I was shocked. There was no way Nancy should have colon cancer. She'd been a vegetarian forever, vegan for many years, no sugar, no caffeine, no alcohol, no drugs. Ever.

Can purity cause cancer? Can stress about eating perfectly cause cancer? Of course not. It's just the luck of the draw. Or possible exposure to Round Up. Nancy's theory.

The weather had turned nasty. California drought-times nasty, anyway. Mid 40s with light scattered showers. The sky had darkened and the wind had whipped through the trees, clogging the gutters with piles of colorful leaves. It almost made me believe that the natural order of the seasons had been restored.

I decided to drive down to Santa Maria, where Nancy was staying with her brother's family, to give her moral support, and to assess how she was really doing. She'd been texting me that she was suffering PTSD after the surgery, that it felt like a war had been waged in her guts.

Fortunately, her sister-in-law also texted me. *The mass was cancerous but encapsulated so the doctor believes with some chemo she will make a full recovery!!!!* Smiley faces and exuberant fireworks emojis.

My heart leapt. Then Nancy texted me that she wouldn't do chemo. She believed her cure lay in a forty-two-day juice fast, no sugar or protein, combined with regular sits in a hyperbaric oxygen chamber, ingesting special herbal mixes and other natural treatments. I really hoped she was right.

As twisted luck, or perverse serendipity, would have it, the only audio book on my phone during the drive was *Embracing the Unknown: Life Lessons from the Tibetan Book of the Dead*, by Pema Chödrön. I'd picked this book a week or so earlier because it had been four years since my mother died and I still needed closure. I'd been telling myself that writing my book would bring closure, but it hadn't. It had only elongated the need, dulling the pain, but also preventing it from going away. It was in this state of mind that the Pema Chödrön book got my attention while browsing the audio book selections at the Berkeley Public Library.

The sky was full of large puffy cumulus clouds floating past like detached icebergs. The previous night's rain had washed some of the crud out of the air and the sky was a deep cheerful blue. Freeway driving pushed away all worries and anxieties. Nothing more concerning than staying alert and anticipating the actions of other vehicles.

Pema Chödrön's calm voice and her easy-going humor sunk into my consciousness, helping me relax into the drive, making me chuckle a few times even, then it began to frighten me. I had hoped that Pema Chödrön would help me come to terms with my mother's death, but instead she kept pushing my thoughts toward Nancy. How she might have to navigate the bardo—the realm between one life and the next—all too soon.

Nancy was only 60 years old. Even her alcoholic and abusive father lived to be 79. Based on that fact alone Nancy should live to be 90 or even 100.

Thirty or forty minutes later, I was so overwhelmed by what Pema Chödrön was saying that I turned the audio book off, preferring to stare at the California landscape without any background narration. Massive farms. Impoverished laborers. Ominous gray sky. Smudgy silhouette of the coastal range. Highway 101 retraces the Spanish Camino Real, the long road that the Catholic fathers built to connect the Missions. Every few miles I passed a replica Mission bell on an oversized shepherd's staff and thought about all the slaughtered native Californian's who were betrayed by that bell, by those stories and prayers.

I really wish I had turned Pema Chödrön off much sooner. Before I heard her insist, demon like, fiercely with diamond-slitted eyes, that the dead need the living to help them navigate from this world to the next. She said it's easier for the dead if they can remain in a familiar place, with people they know and love. And most importantly, she said, the dead need to hear a human voice speaking to them, reading to them, guiding them through the tricky options presented in the bardo. She said, do not let go of your dead too early or they will become lost.

South of Salinas, it hit me hard just how much I had failed my mother by honoring her wish to donate her body to science. I felt sick to my stomach and wanted to pull over.

If my mother hadn't been rushed out of our house in a dark van, if I had read to her instead, while her body rested in Paula's office, maybe my mother would have safely made her way through the bardo, and a channel of communication could have opened between us.

I stopped in a placeless place to pee and buy a bag of chips. I got gas and watched other people getting gas. Everyone I saw going in and out of the convenience store was distorted. Their eyes pushed in or popped out. Their foreheads compressed or dented like cans. Their ears twisted away from their heads. I noticed a car with the hood propped open. A van with the doors torn off, crammed full of boxes and plastic bags. Tweakers hustled over like crabs asking me for money. I shoved the pump back in its cradle. Put the cap on and hurried off.

The long descent out of San Luis Obispo leads straight to Pismo Beach. A few miles away from the ocean, I still felt like a complete failure of a son. Then the ocean leapt through the windshield and I sat bolt upright, ten-times more relaxed and at peace than I had felt all day. I really wanted to stop. Sneak in a twenty-minute walk along the soft white beach. But I thought of Nancy and kept going.

I parked next to her brother's house. The front yard was full of fall / Halloween / Thanksgiving decorations. A wooden bridge crossed a stone creek. Two flags flopped around on a flagpole. The Stars and Stripes and a black and white POW/MIA flag.

Nancy answered the door with a bright smile on her face. Her hair was thick and long. She was wearing baggy stretch pants and a Guatemalan top. I had to remind myself that she was 60-years-old. She looked like she could be 40.

Nancy and I had a deep connection, but in many ways we were opposites. She was intuitive, while I was analytical. She was brave; I was careful. She took the difficult path. I was like my mother, looking for the easy way out. In some ways, Nancy and my mother were also kindred souls. Both outwardly social, both curious and inquisitive and judgmental. Both with rapid fire minds. The big difference between them was that Nancy never had kids. She never had to exchange her skin for someone else's skin. Her bones for someone else's bones. That and my mother was a hedonist, a pleasure seeker, like me, while Nancy had always been on the path of knowledge and understanding.

Nancy's brother was cooking black beans and rice in the kitchen, wearing a Tulane University football jersey. Nancy called him Bro. He called her Sis. His son came in the front door and called Nancy, Auntie Veggie Burger, on his way to his room.

We excused ourselves and sat in the living room. The walls were covered with Native American regalia. A feather head-dress. A beaded mask. A tomahawk. There were shelves full of pestle and mortar, bowls, and arrowheads. There were two large safes full of guns.

Nancy explained to me how she spent almost three hours a day juicing; and drove to Santa Barbara two or three days a week to sit in the hyperbaric chamber; and how she went somewhere else for vitamin C transfusions; and she was walking two or three miles a day with the dog. She was exhausted, she complained. But she was managing. And she felt a lot better.

By the time I left a couple days later, I knew Nancy was in good hands. Her brother would do everything possible to help her. Her brother's wife was like a sister-mother. A fierce protector.

Half an hour later I stopped at Avila Beach to decompress. The minute I stepped out of the car I felt the calming effect of the ocean air, the light, the steady variability of crashing waves.

I got a coffee at Kraken Café and carried it past a large group of elderly ladies sketching the facades of the seafront businesses. I took my shoes and socks off. The sand was cool. The surf shockingly cold. The bright sunlight sparkling on the water played tricks with my eyes. Painful and beautiful. Like a wall of mirrors expanding the tiny, almost hidden beach, into the infinite.

My mother hated Fresno. Fresno was her dead end. Her one-way bridge to nowhere. She thought she was taking a short trip to visit the in-laws, and that she would return to real life in Laguna Beach in a week or so. Then my father died unexpectedly—heart attack—and she was stuck. Stranded in a town she never liked. A 29-year-old widowed mother without a job.

Fresno may only be 275 miles from Laguna Beach. But the tectonic plates of her life had shifted and left a gaping hole. Beach town California may as well have slid into the ocean and vanished. Her life with my father had been volatile and frightening, but it was also exciting. Her life in Fresno became a slow grind. The grind of going to work five days a week, the grind of raising a kid, the grind of running a house, shopping, cleaning, paying bills, etc., etc., etc.

The beach became a dream. A someday thing. The place she imagined being when she needed to be somewhere else. Someday. After you move out, she'd tell me. Someday. When I have some money saved. Someday. When my dues are paid and I'm free to go. I'll live in a bungalow, or an apartment, or a trailer in Cambria, or Morrow Bay, or Cayucos.

I trudged across the sand to the stairs leading back up to the street, pausing for a moment to watch a group of vultures peck away at something dead on the beach, maybe a seal. Five or six of them seemed to be talking things over between bites. One of the vultures turned its head in my direction, beat its wings two or three times, rising a foot or so in the air, before resting its weight back on the sand. Like it was shrugging its shoulders. Like it was saying, Hey, what do you expect?

I stumbled when I got to the top of the stairs and fell on the pavement. I took a moment to catch my breath and to determine if I had hurt myself. There was a squat blocky hotel with American flags on every balcony across the street. Up the hill to the right, past a row of ocean front homes, was a bluff covered in scrub with a trail heading down to the beach. I walked the other way, toward the long pier, which was now fenced off, damaged by the last big storm, past the clan of biddy artists, each striving to capture her own vision of the thin California light.

Out of habit, I looked for my mother. After four years, I didn't really expect to see her, or hear her, or sense her. But for some reason, I kept looking.

Maybe, I decided, with a sense of relief, it was finally time for me to accept my little slice of reality for what it was. Severely limited to the here and now. Locked in its three-dimensional predictability. A narrow tunnel burrowing straight through time, without any mystical funny business.

I turned and took one more look at the ocean. The damaged pier. The gathering of the black-winged monks. No matter what happens with this book, I realized walking back to my car, it will always be a poor substitute for the tree I didn't plant, for the memorial I didn't give, for the obituary I didn't write.

Pema Chödrön's lectures on the *Tibetan Book of the Dead* have made one thing perfectly clear, however. I am going to amend my death wishes to explicitly state that I do not want to donate my body to science. That I should not be taken from my home before my family and close friends remove my clothes, wash my body, shave my face, wrap me in clean cloth, and read to me as I pass on to whatever wherever. Let there be a simple vigil, then the vastness of flames.

I toss my coffee cup in a trashcan, then get back in my car and drive slowly up the hill. Away from the ocean. Back home to Berkeley.

LIST OF PHOTOGRAPHS

The images at the beginning of the chapters were exhumed from boxes of my mother's family photos. Except for numbers seven and eight, which I took myself.

—*TL*

#1 - p 15, *Childhood on Vacation*, Michigan 1930s

#2 - p 37, *Before the Golden Gate*, San Francisco, 2013

#3 - p 89, *Now There is Three*, Southern California, 1959

#4 - p 115, *At the Office*, Fresno, 1980s

#5 - p 139, *Sun Worshiper*, Southern California, 1950s

#6 - p 157, *Kitchen Greeting*, Fresno, 1970s

#7 - p 179, *Postcard from Cabbage Town*, Atlanta, 2009

#8 - p 203, *Last Day*, Berkeley, 2015

About the Author

Thoreau Lovell is originally from Fresno, California. He currently lives in Berkeley, with his wife, their two dogs and cat. He previously worked in the library at San Francisco State University as a technology and collection access administrator. Currently, he's the publisher and co-founder of Wet Cement Press. He has published two books of poetry, *Amnesia's Diary* (Ex Nihilo Press) and *Wilson Wiley Variations* (Wet Cement Press). The obscure mystery writer B.E. Lovell is his father. More info at ThoreauLovell.com

www.ingramcontent.com/pod-product-compliance
Lightning Source LLC
Chambersburg PA
CBHW031522310726
48971CB00008B/2323